A BAD PLA

Dyan Sheldon is known throughout the world for her numerous books for children and adults. As an adult author, she has been described as one of todays funniest woman writers. Some of her children's books include: *A Witch Got on at Paddington Station*, *The Garden*, *Harry and Chicken* series, *My Brother is a Visitor From Another Planet*, *Tall Thin and Blonde* and in Young Piper, *Lilah's Monster*.

Dyan Sheldon regularly visits London, enjoys travelling the world by motorbike and lives the rest of the year in New York with her cats.

Dyan Sheldon

A BAD PLACE FOR A BUS STOP

A Piper Original
PAN MACMILLAN
CHILDREN'S BOOKS

First published 1994 by Pan Macmillan Children's Books

a division of Pan Macmillan Publishers Limited
Cavaye Place, London SW10 9PG
and Basingstoke

Associated companies throughout the world

ISBN 0 330 33016 0

Copyright © Dyan Sheldon 1994

The right of Dyan Sheldon to be identified as the
author of this work has been asserted by her in accordance
with the Copyright, Designs and Patents Act 1988.

3 5 7 9 8 6 4

A CIP catalogue record for this book is available from
the British Library

Typeset by CentraCet Limited, Cambridge
Printed and bound in Great Britain by
Cox & Wyman Ltd, Reading, Berkshire

A BAD PLACE
FOR A
BUS STOP

CHAPTER ONE

A Bad Place for a Bus Stop

'Stop!' shouted Mrs Preski. 'Stop! Stop! Stop!'

Dana stopped. She'd been concentrating very hard on the chord change and keeping her elbow bent, as Mrs Preski had instructed, but now she looked over. Mrs Preski was holding her hands to her ears.

'Wasn't that right?' asked Dana glumly.

This wasn't really a question. Dana could tell from the way Mrs Preski's lips were all bunched together that it hadn't been right. She sighed. It never was.

Today was Thursday. Thursdays were Dana's least favourite day of the week, because on Thursdays Dana had her cello lesson with Mrs Preski after school. Dana wasn't too fond of either Mrs Preski or the cello. Mrs Preski was a tall, precise woman with short grey curls, beady brown eyes, and skin the colour of evaporated milk. She was very neat, and always wore a straight beige skirt, a starched white blouse and a beige cardigan. Dana was sure that it couldn't be the same skirt, blouse and cardigan week after week, but it was hard to tell. The cello was almost as big as Dana herself, and though it was badly scratched from having been left out of its case too many times, it was the deep, warm colour of chestnuts. Mrs Preski and the cello felt the same about Dana as she felt about them.

Mrs Preski was staring at her as though she'd just said something truly amazing.

'Right?' asked Mrs Preski. She removed her hands from her ears and folded them behind her back. 'Right?'

Dana moved so that she was directly behind her cello.

Mrs Preski started pacing back and forth. Dana hated it when Mrs Preski started pacing back and forth because it meant she was in for another lecture about practising and paying attention. She glanced at her watch. It was five twenty-five. Mrs Preski always gave her a lecture about practising and paying attention every Thursday at five twenty-five.

Mrs Preski came to a halt in front of Dana and her cello. 'Let me ask you a question, Dana Bindle,' said Mrs Preski coldly. 'Was one trying to play Beethoven just then, or was one trying to impersonate the sound of a cat having its tail pulled?'

'Beethoven?' said Dana hopefully.

Mrs Preski didn't think so. 'Guess again,' said Mrs Preski.

What a dumb place for a bus stop, Dana was thinking as she trudged down Shroder Drive through the snow, her cello in her arms. *It's miles from anywhere*.

One of the things Dana hated about Thursdays, besides her lesson and Mrs Preski's lectures, was carrying her cello. She had to lug her cello all the way to school with her in the morning. Then she had to lug it all the way to Mrs Preski's in the afternoon. And then she had to lug it back home again. Dana found the whole process extremely tiring.

Thinking of how tiring it all was, especially in the

2

snow, Dana came to a stop in the middle of Shroder Drive with a weary sigh. Icy flakes flew in her eyes and up her nostrils.

'You'd think Mrs Preski could at least live near the bus stop,' Dana grumbled.

But Mrs Preski, of course, did not live near the bus stop. She lived as far away from the bus stop as she could get.

Dana sighed again. She looked around, just to make sure that Mrs Preski wasn't following her, checking to see if she was doing something wrong. Mrs Preski was always checking up on Dana, and when she did she usually caught her doing something wrong.

The road was empty. Dana carefully lowered the cello to the ground. Dana was pretty sure that Mrs Preski would consider dragging one's cello through the snow wrong, but Dana was too tired to care. She took a deep breath and began to drag, very slowly and gently at first, and then a little faster and harder. Behind her, the cello left a trail rather like that of a giant snail. It glistened in the street lights.

'I don't even like cellos,' Dana complained as she ploughed on. 'I like guitars.'

This, too, was true. Dana didn't like cellos. She thought they were old-fashioned and dead boring. Cellos, it seemed to Dana, were meant to be played by someone older than twelve; someone with grey hair who wore a long beige skirt and a starched white blouse. Someone who enjoyed playing music that put Dana to sleep. Dana wanted to play music that was fun. She wanted to wear bright clothes and dance on stage. She wanted an electric guitar; one

3

with a red face and chrome trim. If she had an electric guitar she would never forget to practise or to put it back in its case. Mrs Preski said that the electric guitar was not a musical instrument, but an instrument of torture. Dana's parents believed in culture. They wanted Dana to play Schubert and Mozart not rhythm and blues and rock and roll.

Huffing and puffing, Dana came to the corner of Shroder and Newton. She stopped again, squinting through the thickly falling snow. Should she go left or right?

Dana always got confused here, even when it was possible to see where you were going. Not only did Mrs Preski live miles from the bus stop, but she lived in one of those neighbourhoods that are nothing but row upon row of identical houses on identical streets. Terraces, Dana's mother called them. Dana thought it was more like a hall of mirrors than a terrace. Sometimes Dana would walk right past Mrs Preski's door, and then get told off for being late. Going home was no better. On one occasion she had gone round in a circle and ended up back at Mrs Preski's instead of at the bus stop. 'It's because you don't pay attention,' Mrs Preski had told her. 'With life as with your cello lessons.'

Left, Dana decided. Left on Newton, right on Albert. She tightened her grip on the cello and moved on.

The bus stop was deserted. Dana looked down the road. All she could see were a few distant lights. None of them seemed to be moving towards her. She stood herself and her cello against the shelter, and waited. While she waited she thought about how

4

nice it would be if there were a bus stop right outside Mrs Preski's door. Then she could wait inside, where it was warm, instead of outside where it was freezing cold.

It'd be even better if there were a fish and chip shop behind the bus stop, Dana told herself, continuing her thought. She could be standing in the lighted doorway right this minute, eating a packet of chips while she waited for the bus, instead of standing all alone in the dark with snow seeping through her shoes.

A little afraid that Mrs Preski might be right, and that she didn't always pay the proper amount of attention, Dana stepped to the kerb and looked down the road again. There was nothing there but those distant lights, but now there seemed to be less than before. Dana's stomach growled. It was almost time for supper. Her mother would be setting the table right about now. Dana's meal would be nearly ready.

I'll never get home in time at this rate, thought Dana. *It'll be cold and dried out by the time I get back.*

'This is a very bad place for a bus stop, if you ask me,' said a deep, loud voice behind her.

Dana turned round. There, at the other end of the shelter, was a very small woman with six very large paper carrier bags. She was the most extraordinary-looking woman Dana had ever seen. She had strong, sharp features and dark brown skin. Her black hair was done in dozens of plaits. At the end of each plait was a tiny gold star. In the dim light of the bus shelter, it almost looked as though her enormous eyes were golden, too.

Dana's mother was forever telling her never to speak to strangers. Dana was never sure why. It seemed to her that if you never spoke to strangers you would never make any new friends, or get directions, or buy a packet of sweets. In any case, Dana was so surprised to discover that she wasn't alone, that she completely forgot all the advice her mother had given her about never speaking to strangers, and said the first thing that came into her head.

'Why, I was thinking that only a little while ago,' said Dana.

'Of course you were,' said the woman. 'Great minds think alike, don't they? That's why we're together.' She extended her hand. 'Lup,' she said.

Dana didn't understand what 'That's why we're together' meant, so she ignored it.

'Pardon?' asked Dana. She stared down at the hand. It was wearing what looked very much like a gardening glove. Dana had never seen anyone wear gardening gloves in the snow before.

'Lup,' the woman repeated. 'Liski Lup. *When things are down, that's when I'm up.*'

'Oh,' said Dana. She shook the hand in the canvas glove. The glove was decorated with dancing garden gnomes. Dana wasn't quite sure what to say next, so she did what she always did on such occasions – she said nothing.

'And you?' prompted Liski Lup. 'What are you called?'

Dana flushed. She was always being told off for not remembering her manners. 'Dana,' she said politely. 'Dana Bindle.'

'Dana Bindle . . .' Liski Lup tilted her head as though thinking this over. The gold stars twinkled.

'What an unusual name,' she said at last. She frowned. 'Very unusual. I can't say I've ever come across it before.' She sounded disapproving.

'I can't say I've ever come across anyone called Liski Lup before either,' said Dana.

Liski Lup acted as if Dana hadn't spoken. 'I hope the bus comes soon,' said Liski Lup, looking down the road in the wrong direction. She gave herself a shake and the stars tinkled again. 'I hate the cold, as I'm sure you do, too,' she continued, turning back to Dana. 'You and I weren't made for this climate. And, of course, the snow is so peculiar, too, don't you think? It reminds me of Quargian dandruff. Does it remind you of Quargian dandruff?'

Quargian dandruff? Dana opened her mouth to answer, but no words came out. She stared at Liski Lup. Liski Lup was talking about Quargian dandruff and wearing fuzzy pink ear muffs and a long purple overcoat. Under the overcoat was a rather pretty silver party dress with a deep ruffle around the hem. Under that were woolly red tights. She had blue Doc Martens on her feet and dangling gold earrings made up of very small stars in her ears. *Snow isn't the only thing that's peculiar*, thought Dana.

Liski caught a flake of snow on the tip of her thumb. 'Still,' she said, 'best not to complain. You know what they say, *She who complains gets left in the rains*.' She clapped Dana on the shoulder. 'And besides, if it weren't for the snow I might not have found you so easily, might I?'

Dana was sure she was paying attention now, but still she couldn't follow the conversation. 'Might you what?' asked Dana.

'Found you so easily.' Liski Lup pointed behind Dana to where her footprints and the furrow made by the cello led to the shelter. 'That was clever thinking,' she said. 'Very clever. You left a perfect trail.'

Dana was not used to being praised for her clever thinking. She liked it. *Clever*, she repeated to herself. *Very clever and perfect.*

She was still repeating the words 'clever' and 'very' and 'perfect' to herself when Liski Lup suddenly shouted out, 'The bus! There's the bus!' She quickly gathered up her bags. 'Hurry!' she ordered. 'Pick up that whateveryoucallit and get on board.'

Dana had been so busy enjoying being very clever and perfect that she hadn't heard or seen a bus approaching. Not wanting to get left behind, she picked up her cello as directed, and turned to face the road.

Just drawing to a stop by the kerb was a large black object, flecked with silver. Hundreds of minuscule lights were wrapped around it like a belt. In shape it resembled a rather thick hamburger. It smelled a bit like a hamburger, too.

'But that's not a bus,' said Dana.

The gold stars tinkled. 'Of course it's a bus,' said Liski Lup. 'What else would it be?' She laughed. 'It's not a Shavellian limousine, is it?'

Quargian dandruff . . . Shavellian limousines . . . Buses that looked like hamburgers . . . Dana really wished she knew what Liski Lup was talking about.

'Well, no,' said Dana. 'No, I don't suppose it does.' Perhaps the bus only looked like a hamburger because she was so hungry. So hungry and so cold.

The door opened. A sudden blast of hot air melted the snow into puddles at her feet.

Liski Lup put one foot on the stairs. She turned. 'Come on, Dana Bindle!' she shouted. *'Don't be late, my little mate. Time and space don't ever wait.'* And with that she vanished inside.

Dana raised her face to the heat that was coming from the bus in waves. She stared at the comforting light that shone from within. The snow was getting heavier. The night was very dark. Who knew how long Dana might have to wait for a proper-looking bus?

I might have to wait ages, Dana told herself. *My parents will be really worried. And I still have homework to do. And my supper will be ruined by the time I get home.*

Sure that she was doing the right thing, Dana picked up her cello and followed Liski Lup on board.

CHAPTER TWO

One Good Reason Why You Should Never Speak to Strangers

Dana thought of a very good reason for never speaking to strangers the instant the door closed behind her with a businesslike clunk. The driver was a robot. He looked rather like a suit of shimmery blue armour with flashing red eyes. Dana held up her bus pass, but he didn't even glance at it.

'Step back!' he ordered in a flat, empty voice. 'Step back!'

'I haven't done the right thing at all,' Dana muttered to herself as she stepped back. 'I've done the wrong thing again.'

She stopped once she was away from the driver and looked around. Dana's heart sank the way her father's golf ball had sunk the time she accidentally hit it into the lake.

The bus looked less like a bus on the inside than it did on the outside. There weren't any other passengers. Instead of the orderly rows of seats that most buses had, this one had chairs of all shapes and sizes stuck every which way. Chairs large enough for a pair of elephants who insisted on sitting together, and chairs small enough for a twelve-year-old girl who was a little on the small side. There was even a chair that was the perfect size and shape for Dana's cello.

Dana's eyes moved to the walls. Dana was used

to walls that were white, or perhaps a muted shade of pink, yellow or blue. Dana had been amazed the first time she saw Mrs Preski's bathroom, which was covered with shiny wallpaper decorated with fish and shells. But Mrs Preski's fish and shells were dull and ordinary next to the interior of Liski Lup's bus. The walls were painted in swirls of colour and blotches of patterns that shimmered and glowed.

Not only did the walls of the bus remind Dana of a kaleidoscope, but there were hooks and rings and shelves and baskets attached to it everywhere. But no windows. Who had ever heard of a bus without windows? How did you know when you'd come to your stop?

Something over her head caught Dana's eye. She looked towards the ceiling. There was a window; the window was the roof. Dana watched the clouds approaching rapidly. She thought about this. If the clouds were approaching, then either the sky was falling or they weren't going forward, as any other bus would be doing, they were going up.

We can't be going up, Dana reassured herself. *That's impossible. Buses don't fly*.

Something below her caught Dana's eye. She looked down. The floor was also a window.

Dana's heart sunk some more, just as her father's golf club had sunk into the lake when she tried to get the ball out with it.

This was impossible, too, of course, but the roofs, the television antennae, the satellite dishes, and the tree-tops were growing smaller and smaller and farther away. Yes, she had definitely done the wrong

11

thing. Possibly because she hadn't been paying enough attention again.

Why did I ever talk to Liski Lup? wondered Dana, wiping sweat from her forehead. Instead of being cold and draughty like a great many buses, this one was hotter than a gas fire. *Why didn't I listen to my mum?*

'Well, here we are, safe and warm!' cried Liski Lup.

Dana turned round. She'd been so busy taking in the chairs and the walls and the ceiling and the floor that she'd lost track of Liski.

Liski Lup had removed her ear muffs and her overcoat and had dumped all her bags on an enormous metallic-green armchair. In the light of the bus, Dana could see that her hair was plum, not black, but that her eyes were definitely gold. She was pulling something out of one of her bags.

'Welcome aboard, Dana Bindle,' boomed Liski Lup. She handed Dana a card.

The card was black. In silver lettering it said:

Liski Lup
Intergalactic Trouble Shooter Grade Z
No Problem Too Big or Too Small

Dana gazed at the card for a few seconds, not sure what to make of it. Exactly what was an Intergalactic Trouble Shooter? She looked at her companion, whose dress, Dana now saw, seemed to be made of coloured aluminium foil. The Doc Martens were covered with tiny maps of the stars. There was something that looked remarkably like a bunch of carrots sticking out of her pocket.

I guess *that's* an Intergalactic Trouble Shooter, she told herself. Not that that answered her question. She still didn't know what one was.

Liski Lup was rummaging frantically through her other bags. 'I'm certainly glad we made this bus,' said Liski. 'Ah! There you are!' She triumphantly pulled out a large floral scarf and started to wrap it around her head. 'The next bus to Wadric-5 isn't for another twenty Earth years,' she added.

'Wadric-5?' echoed Dana. 'Twenty *Earth* years?'

This was what happened when you spoke to strangers. This was what happened when you didn't pay attention. If her parents found out about this, they were going to be even madder than Mrs Preski was when Dana forgot to practise. This was definitely much more serious than losing the golf club in the lake. 'But I don't want to go to Wadric-5,' protested Dana.

'None of us do any more,' said Liski Lup gloomily. 'And with good reason, too. Not even the least sensible Wadrickians want to be on Wadric-5. Not the way things are now. But you know what they say, *duty doesn't call, it shouts.*'

She removed a large paper fan from one of her bags and began to wave it back and forth in front of her face. 'At least this time they finally gave me a little help,' she said sourly. The fan flapped back and forth faster and faster. 'You have no idea how difficult it is when you have to do everything by yourself.'

'But Miss Lup . . .' began Dana.

Liski held the fan. 'Ms, not Miss,' she said shortly. '*I never miss, my lasers whizz, and that is why they call me Ms.*'

Dana decided not to think about lasers. 'Ms Lup,' Dana corrected herself. 'I can't go to Wadric-5. I have to be back on Hollyrod Drive in time for supper.'

Liski Lup eyed Dana over the pair of canvas sandals she'd just removed from a Woolworth's carrier bag. 'Hollyrod Drive? Why in the cosmos would you want to go to Hollyrod Drive? I'll bet it's duller than a dead star.'

Dana wasn't sure if Hollyrod Drive was duller than a dead star or not, but the suggestion that it was made her feel a little defensive. After all, on Hollyrod Drive they had cable TV and a tree that had been cut in half by lightning during a storm. She was sure there wouldn't be anything like that on a dead star.

'Because I live there,' said Dana a little more sharply than she'd intended.

Liski Lup gave her a look. It was long, appraising, thoughtful sort of look.

'Now let me get this straight,' she said. 'Are you telling me that you never had any intention of going to Wadric-5? Are you telling me that you do, in time as well as space, really live on Hollyrod Drive? Is that what you're telling me?'

Dana nodded. 'Yes,' she said. 'That's what I'm telling you.'

Ms Lup pointed one long canvas-covered finger at Dana. 'Now let me get this straight,' she said. 'Are you trying to tell me that you are *not* an apprentice Intergalactic Trouble Shooter, but a *human* child?'

Dana frowned. Liski Lup didn't make being human sound like a particularly good thing. 'Of course I'm human,' said Dana. 'What else could I be?'

Liski Lup glared at Dana as though she'd never heard anyone say anything that dumb before.

'You *could* be a junior cosmic ranger from Borio who is dedicated to fighting negativity and evil and keeping the universe free, that's what you *could* be,' said Liski darkly. 'You *could* be my trusty sidekick. You could be the help I was promised.'

'But I'm not,' Dana pointed out. 'I'm—'

'You're a human child who lives on Hollyrod Drive.'

'Yes,' said Dana. 'Yes, that's it exactly. I'm a human child and I live on Hollyrod Drive.'

Liski Lup pointed a sandal at Dana. The sandal was neon pink. 'Then perhaps you'd be good enough to tell me what you were doing at that bus stop with a Beda-X Dematerializer if you're not an apprentice Intergalactic Trouble Shooter?' she demanded. She tossed the sandal across the room. 'Hey, Dana Bindle? Answer me that! Why did you leave that trail for me if you're not from Borlo?'

'But I didn't leave a trail,' Dana protested. 'And it isn't a Beda-X whatever you said. It's a cello.'

'Don't be ridiculous,' snapped Liski Lup. She yanked the carrots out of her pocket. 'No one with a gluon of sense would drag a cello through the snow like that. It has to be a Beda-X Dematerializer. That's the other thing they're good for, making trails.'

I knew I should have carried the cello, Dana scolded herself. She wasn't sure what a gluon was, but it didn't sound as though it were very large.

'Well, it's not a Beda-X Dematerializer,' said Dana. 'It's my cello. My mother's still making the payments on it.'

Liski Lup was waving the carrots about. 'This is most inconvenient,' she muttered. 'Most inconvenient. The whole mission depends on there being two of us.' She dropped the carrots, and started untying her Doc Martens. 'I should have known it was too good to be true,' she grumbled. 'They always promise me help, but do I ever get it? No, I never get it. *You can do it, Liski,* they say. *You're the best.*' She tossed the star-spangled boots aside. 'I *am* the best, of course,' she went on, 'but that is several light-years beside the point. The point is that I'm always left on my own, no matter how much they promise.' She removed the woolly red tights. Sand spilled onto the floor. 'And I'm tired of it. I'm very, very tired of it.'

Now that the misunderstanding was cleared up, Dana was feeling a little more generous, or at least a little more polite.

'I am sorry,' said Dana. 'I'd love to help you, I really would, but I do have to get home for supper.'

'A human,' said Liski Lup, flinging the tights over the arm of the chair. 'Of all the things to help me, I get a human child. With a cello.' She sighed. 'Still, we'll just have to make the best of it, won't we?'

She turned her face to the sky above them. Dana turned her face to the sky above them, too. It was filled with stars. Some of them were very large. It also seemed to be filled with quite a bit of rubble.

'*If you can't find your shoe, you just have to make do,*' said Liski Lup philosophically.

That golf-club feeling came over Dana again. 'Oh, I didn't mean—'

'Here.' Liski Lup handed her a silver duvet she'd

wrenched from one of the bags. 'You may need this. We pass through some cold spots on this trip.'

Dana blinked at the duvet. It seemed to be glowing. Her stomach rumbled. 'I'm very, very sorry,' said Dana, 'but you don't understand. I can't go to Wadric-5. I have to get home. We'll have to turn round.'

'Turn round?' repeated Liski. 'Sorry?' She shook her head and the stars on the ends of her plaits danced. 'I'm afraid it's you who don't understand, Dana Bindle. We can't turn round. We're in a hurry. The urds are disappearing from Wadric-5 faster than light into a black hole. And it's my job to stop them. The whole future of Wadric-5 is at stake.'

In spite of herself, and her worry about missing supper, Dana was a little curious. 'Urds?' she asked. 'What are urds?'

'That's a human for you.' Liski Lup rolled her eyes. 'Dana Bindle doesn't even know what an urd is!' She pulled off one of her gardening gloves. *If you want to see, just look at me,* she instructed. She held out her hand, palm up.

Dana looked. There were no lines on Liski Lup's palm, her hand was as smooth as a mannequin's. In the very centre of Liski Lup's smooth hand was what appeared to be a tiny television screen. A small, knobbly, multi-coloured creature with a long curling tail and hooded, protruding eyes stared back at her. It had a tiny horn in the middle of its forehead.

Dana jumped back in surprise. 'Why, it's some sort of lizard!' Dana had never cared much for lizards.

The hand closed. 'More or less,' she admitted.

This is too much, thought Dana. *I'm missing my*

supper and I'm going to get in trouble for being late and I'm not going to have time to finish my homework for tomorrow, and all because of some dumb reptile.

'Surely you can take a few minutes to bring me back to the bus stop,' said Dana reasonably. 'After all, what could be so important about a little lizard?'

Liski Lup arched her eyebrows. The colour of her eyes changed from light gold to dark. The effect was not pleasant. 'In my game,' she informed Dana frostily, 'everything's important.'

'But—' bleated Dana.

'*Everything*,' said Liski Lup. 'Even human children.'

Suddenly realizing how tired she was, Dana collapsed into the nearest chair. It was the one that was the right size for a twelve-year-old girl who was slightly small for her age. She looked down at the floor. The Earth had disappeared completely. There was nothing to be seen but thousands upon thousands of moons, stars and planets. None of them seemed too familiar. She flinched as a clump of debris brushed the window.

'Now what am I going to do?' grumbled Dana. If the buses to Wadric-5 only ran every twenty years she might have some trouble getting back to Hollyrod Drive.

'You're going to help me, that's what you're going to do,' said Liski. 'I don't like it any more than you do, believe me. I've worked with humans before.' Something clicked into place. '*But there's no time for wishin' when Lup has a mission*, you know.' Something snapped. Liski sighed happily.

Dana looked up. Liski Lup, dressed now in a shiny

18

lilac jump suit and the pink canvas sandals, was hanging by her feet from a ring on the wall. She was sound asleep.

Dana sat back, all at once aware that the temperature in the bus had already dropped by quite a few degrees. She pulled the duvet up to her chin. At the front of the bus, the robot made bleeping sounds whenever something nearly crashed into the windscreen. Feeling a little lonely, Dana leaned over and laid her head on her cello.

CHAPTER THREE

No One with a Gluon of Sense Goes to Earth Except to Shop

If Dana Bindle had got on the right bus, rather than the wrong bus, she would have driven home through quiet, tree-lined streets with houses that all looked very much the same. She would have passed the rows of shops on the high street and might even have seen one of her mother's friends wheeling a pushchair through the crowds. Her mind would probably have wandered while they rolled along. She might have thought about supper, or what had happened at school, or whether or not she could skip her cello practice tonight since she'd already played for over an hour. She might even have thought about today's lecture from Mrs Preski about working hard and using her brain for a change. Though maybe not. Maybe she would have daydreamed about playing the guitar in a rock-and-roll band instead.

Dana Bindle, however, did not get on the right bus, she got on the wrong bus. As a result, she sat huddled in her duvet as the temperature continued to drop, Liski Lup snored and the driver bleeped. Dana stared down at the floor, her heart sinking like a bag full of golf clubs thrown over a bridge.

There were no tree-lined streets and no neat houses up here. There were no rows of shops. There were no friends of her mother's strolling through the stars. There was only space, space and more space.

It was crowded and empty at the same time. Things moved at such speed, and so randomly, that the bus was always tilting and swerving, bucking through showers of meteors and bumping through clouds of gases. It was most unnerving.

'What if I never get home?' Dana asked aloud. 'What if I'm stuck on Wadric-5 for ever?'

At the front of the bus, the robot started to whirr. Dana looked over at him. His head was spinning around. She hadn't been hurtling through space for more than a few hours, but she already knew that this was not a good sign. A large object that looked rather like the moon with the lights turned out was heading for the windscreen. *Whirrrrrrrbleepbleepbleepbleepbleep*, said the driver. Dana closed her eyes. She screamed.

'If you want to be an assistant Intergalactic Trouble Shooter you're going to have to get over that for a start,' said Liski Lup. 'Intergalactic Trouble Shooters never show fear. As the ITS motto says, *While others cry, our cheeks are dry.*'

'But I don't want to be an assistant Intergalactic Trouble Shooter,' said Dana. She opened her eyes. A fraction of a second ago, Liski Lup had been hanging on the wall, sound asleep. Now she was settling into the chair across from Dana, heaving a couple of carrier bags onto her lap.

Ms Lup ignored Dana. 'And as for spending the rest of your life on Wadric-5,' she continued. 'I'll have you know that though it may not be what it once was, it's still a whole lot better than that insignificant little galactic suburb you call home.'

At first, Dana thought she must mean Hollyrod

Drive. 'That's not true,' said Dana. 'Hollyrod Drive isn't insignificant. We have a tree that was struck by lightning.'

The bus started bouncing up and down. Liski Lup gave her a look that said quite clearly, *Lightning: big deal*. 'I wasn't talking about Hollyrod Drive,' she said testily, 'though I'm sure it's insignificant, too. I was talking about your puny planet.'

Dana couldn't hide her surprise. 'You mean *Earth*?' She had never heard anyone call the Earth insignificant before. Everyone she knew thought the Earth was very significant.

'Of course I mean Earth.' She started removing things from the bags and putting them on the floor. 'This is a complex, sophisticated universe. How many tiny, insignificant galactic suburbs do you think there are?'

Dana fidgeted. *Not that many, I guess.*

'The only things you've done that anyone would notice is to blare rock-and-roll music through the galaxy and throw your rubbish around.'

'I don't think that's totally fair,' said Dana.

She searched her mind for something to say in the Earth's defence. Dana's class had studied the planets last autumn. It was true that the Americans had sent up a space capsule that played Chuck Berry. It was true that there was quite a bit of human debris drifting among the stars. But Dana was sure that, despite this, Mrs Glashow, her teacher, thought the Earth was significant. If only Dana could remember something Mrs Glashow had said in its favour. At last she thought of something.

22

'The Earth is very important,' Dana answered, 'it's the only planet in its solar system that supports life.'

Liski Lup started laughing so hard that a bunch of bananas and several mangoes fell out of her hands.

'Who told you that?' she demanded. 'Someone on Earth?'

'Of course it was someone on Earth,' said Dana, partially distracted by the apples and oranges Liski Lup was taking from her bag.

'And what do they know?' she asked, tossing a pineapple into the air. 'Hey, Dana Bindle? What do they know? *Where you are is where you are, and when you look you don't see far.*'

'Intelligent life,' said Dana. 'The Earth supports intelligent life.'

Liski laughed some more. 'That's what you think.' She put down tomatoes, carrots and yellow peppers. 'Have you ever heard that old Oppolonian saying?'

'Which one?' asked Dana.

Sarcasm was wasted on Ms Liski Lup.

'*What's smart on Earth is sleep on Oppolonia.*' She found this very funny as well.

Dana knew that you weren't meant to argue with adults – and she did assume that Liski Lup was an adult something – but she was beginning to find her attitude very annoying.

'We're smart,' she said, clutching the sides of her chair as the bus began bouncing harder. 'We have computers, and satellite television, and motor cars, and planes, and spaceships, and—'

'And have you ever wondered why you have so few visitors?'

23

'Pardon?'

'Visitors,' repeated Liski Lup, dumping a bag of nuts, several avocados and a head of lettuce with the other foods. 'Haven't you ever wondered why hardly anyone ever visits your planet?'

Dana hadn't been aware that hardly anyone ever visited her planet. She wondered if this were another example of her inattention. 'They don't?'

'Of course not,' said Liski. 'That's what made it the ideal spot to collect my assistant. No one would ever think of looking for us there.'

Dana wanted to hear as little about Liski Lup's assistant as possible. 'But why don't they visit?' she asked, steering the conversation back to tourists. 'Is it the oxygen?'

'Oxygen schmoxygen,' chanted Liski. She pointed a handful of green beans at Dana. 'The reason no one ever visits your little planet is because there's only one thing to do on Earth.'

'Watch television?' guessed Dana.

Liski Lup shook her head; the tiny stars collided. 'Everyone else got bored with television eons ago.'

'Play golf?' ventured Dana. Dana's father once went all the way to Arizona in the United States to play golf. Of course, that was when he still had a full set of clubs.

'Golf?' The stars on her hair flashed. 'Never heard of it,' said Liski. She spread her hands over the floor. 'This is why.'

'Fruits and vegetables?' A horrible thought occurred to Dana. Her mother was always on at her to eat her fruits and vegetables, did that mean that her mother came from another planet?

'Shopping,' said Liski. 'No one with a gluon of sense would go to Earth for anything else.'

'Shopping?'

Liski nodded. 'Some of the best shopping in the eastern grouping of galaxies. Depending on your interests, of course. It's the last place you'd go for a thermoalboframameter.'

'Shopping?' said Dana again. She'd never thought of the Earth as a shopping mall before, either.

Liski waved her arms. 'Food. . . you do have some wonderful food. Asparagus, mushrooms, papaya, plantains, red cabbage . . .' She reached into one of the bags and pulled out a Cellophane packet. 'And these,' she said. 'I've always been fond of salt and vinegar crisps.'

Dana wasn't too keen on asparagus, but her stomach let out a long low groan at the sight of the crisps. She'd always been fond of them, too.

'Of course, there are those who would disagree with me. You know what they say . . .'

'No,' began Dana, 'I don't know—'.

'*Different features for different creatures*,' said Liski Lup. 'Some go for the flowers or the trees . . .' The golden eyes glowed slightly. 'And some, of course, go for other, less agreeable things . . .'

Dana had been so involved in trying to keep up with the conversation that she'd stopped paying any attention to what was going on in front of the bus. Now, however, she couldn't help but pay attention. A thick, greasy-looking green liquid was being sprayed at the windscreen. The driver was nowhere in sight.

'What's that!' screamed Dana.

Liski looked over her shoulder. 'Water,' said Liski rather enigmatically. She turned back to Dana. 'That doesn't look too good, does it?' she asked.

'It doesn't look like water,' said Dana, still staring at the oily green gunge covering the windscreen.

But Liski Lup was pulling her to the floor. 'Under the seat, Dana Bindle!' she shouted. 'Now!' She grabbed the cello and thrust it into Dana's arms.

Dana's mother had always discouraged her from hiding under furniture, but to her surprise the underside of the seat was like a small well-cushioned cave. No sooner had she squeezed herself and the cello into it than the bus began to roll over and over in a serious way. The lights went out. From somewhere near the controls, the robot went off like a siren.

'What is it?' gasped Dana. 'What's happening?'

'Same old thing,' said Liski through a mouthful of what smelled like banana. 'Pirates.'

The bus was starting to leap and twirl.

'Pirates?' Dana tightened her hold on the cello. 'What pirates?'

'*The* pirates,' snapped Liski. 'Why are we here? What have I been trying to tell you through this entire ride?'

'You haven't been trying to tell me anything,' said Dana crossly as the bus began to rise and dive like a rollercoaster. 'You've been asleep most of the time.'

Liski Lup sighed very loudly. 'You know, Dana Bindle, you really are going to have to pay more attention if you want to be an assistant Intergalactic Trouble Shooter. You really are.'

'But I don't want to be an assistant Intergalactic Trouble Shooter!' cried Dana.

At that moment, the bus hit something hard and stopped. The driver stopped wailing. The lights came back on. Beneath them was something that looked like sand. Above them was a pale green sky.

Liski crawled out from under her seat. 'It's a little late for that, Dana Bindle,' she said. 'You should have told me that before you barged your way onto this bus.' She got to her feet, brushing banana skins from her jumpsuit. 'You're there now. The subatomic particles are in motion. There's no going back.'

'There?' repeated Dana. 'There where?'

'Wadric-5.' Liski started gathering her things together. 'Look sharp!' she ordered, glancing over her shoulder at Dana and her cello, still under the seat. *'She who lingers could lose more than her fingers.'*

Dana looked at her fingers. She hadn't intended to lose them, never mind anything else.

'Hurry up!' shouted Liski Lup. 'There's a lot to be done. Do you remember everything I told you?'

Dana and her cello struggled to a standing position. 'But you haven't told me anything,' panted Dana.

'Nothing?' Liski looked at her suspiciously. 'Nothing at all? Haven't I told you what's happening to the urds?'

Dana shook her head.

'Or about the pirates?'

Dana shook her head again.

'Or about my plan?'

'No,' said Dana, trying not to lose her temper. Even she could see that it wouldn't be wise to argue with the only person you knew on a strange planet. 'You haven't told me anything.'

'Well, that's too bad.' Liski Lup lifted her carrier bags and started towards the exit. 'Because there isn't any time to tell you now.'

CHAPTER FOUR

Dana Discovers When the Next Bus Out of Wadric-5 is Scheduled to Come – and a Few Other Things

Liski Lup opened the bus door and peered out. 'It's all right,' she told Dana in a voice loud enough to be heard over the beeps and hums of the driver. 'The desert is empty. They must have given up in that second whirlpool.'

'Who?' hissed Dana, hovering behind her. 'Who gave up?'

'Don't you listen to anything?' Liski lifted her bags without looking at Dana. 'The pirates, of course.' She hurled herself out of the bus.

Clutching her cello, Dana followed the Intergalactic Trouble Shooter, Grade Z, down the short flight of stairs and into the hot stillness of Wadric-5. The air was chartreuse and mauve, and so thick it seemed possible to hold it in your hand.

As soon as Dana stepped onto the ground, the doors closed behind her and the bus rose so quickly and abruptly that she dropped her cello.

'Schedules,' said Liski Lup, as though offering an explanation.

But Dana wasn't giving Liski her full and undivided attention. She was staring up beyond the disappearing bus and the visible atmosphere to where three violet discs shone in the pale green sky of Wadric-5.

'Schedules?' asked Dana, still looking at the sky. 'Aren't they suns?'

Liski sighed impatiently. 'The bus has a schedule,' she said sharply. 'I have a schedule. You have a schedule. Everything has a schedule. That's the way things work.'

Dana was still taking in her surroundings. The sky was never green and the sun never violet over Hollyrod Drive. Sometimes, in the summer, exhaust fumes hung over the high street like clouds, but most of the time you never knew the air was there.

'I said we all have schedules,' Liski Lup repeated in a booming voice. 'And if we're going to keep to ours, you'd better get these on.'

Dana finally took her eyes from the sky. Liski Lup was pulling two pairs of what looked very much like over-sized ping-pong paddles made in clear amber Perspex out of her bags.

'What are *those*?' asked Dana. Now didn't seem like the right time for a table-tennis game to her, but of course she couldn't be sure. Things were obviously different up here than they were at home.

'Sand shoes,' said Liski simply.

Whenever Mrs Preski answered a question with something Dana didn't understand, Dana would nod and wait to see what happened next. *With Intergalactic Trouble Shooters as with music teachers*, decided Dana. She nodded and waited, watching silently while Liski slipped into a pair of sand shoes, strapping them on with bright pink satin bows.

When she was done, she handed the other pair to Dana.

'You'll need them,' she said.

Dana stared at the sand shoes in her hand. Their bows were blue. It occurred to her that waiting to see what happened might not work as well with Liski Lup as it did with Mrs Preski. She might have to ask questions.

Dana cleared her throat. 'What for?' asked Dana.

'*Use your eyes, don't theorize!*' snapped Liski. She adjusted a pair of silver goggles over her golden eyes. 'You'll need a pair of these, too,' she went on. She reached in another bag and tossed a pair of turquoise goggles to Dana.

Dana used her eyes. Liski Lup had a point, she probably would need the sand shoes and the goggles. There was nothing to be seen in any direction but sand; grey sand and that pale green sky with its violet suns. It was incredibly hot.

'*Move it, mate, we daren't wait*,' boomed Liski.

Dana turned back to her companion. Liski Lup was putting a gigantic hat made out of orange and purple leaves on her head. She wrapped a cape the same grimy colour as the sand around her shoulders. When that was done, she reached into a bag and pulled out another cape and a hat just like hers and handed them to Dana. 'Put these on, too,' ordered Liski. 'They'll keep you from baking and make you inconspicuous from above.'

Inconspicuous? Dana looked at the things Liski Lup had given her to wear: amber ping-pong paddles with royal-blue laces, turquoise racing goggles, a cape the colour of ashes and a hat like a tropical tree. They didn't look very inconspicuous to her. She certainly couldn't wear them on Hollyrod Drive without attracting a crowd.

Dana started to say this to Liski Lup. 'My mum wouldn't let me out of the house dressed like this . . .'; but then she realized that Liski Lup wasn't there. Liski Lup was only a small orange and purple blob in the shimmering distance.

An already familiar voice rolled across the dunes to Dana. *'If you don't hurry, you'll have reason to worry,'* it said.

Dana put on the shoes, the goggles, the hat and the cape as quickly as she could. Then she picked up her cello, and started hurrying after Liski Lup. Dana was beginning to worry. If the next bus *to* Wadric-5 wasn't for twenty years, when was the next bus *off* Wadric-5, she wondered.

How can you have pirates when you don't have an ocean? Dana wondered as she tried to keep her balance on the shifting sands.

There hadn't been so much as a tiny breeze when the bus landed, but now an angry wind swept across the desert of Wadric-5, making it difficult to breathe, difficult to walk, and nearly impossible to see. At least it was making it difficult for *Dana* to breathe, walk and see. Steaming on ahead, however, talking to herself, Liski Lup seemed to have no trouble doing any of these things.

Dana bent her head a little lower, set her mouth a

little more firmly against her cello case to stop sand from getting in it, and trudged on.

'One two, one two,' Dana muttered as she forced her feet to move along. Liski Lup glided over the sand as though it were glass, but Dana still hadn't got the hang of the sand shoes. Sand poured into her shoes and filled up her socks. She was constantly falling over. 'One two, one two,' she repeated. 'One two, one two.'

Not watching what she was doing, Dana tripped over yet another dip and landed sprawling in the sand. She already hated sprawling in the sand more than she hated her lessons with Mrs Preski. Unlike the dry, warm sand of Earth, the sand of Wadric-5 was slimy and cold.

Dana raised her head. 'Wait for me!' she screamed. 'Wait for me!'

Metres away, disappearing and reappearing as the strong winds blew clouds of sand between them, Liski Lup glided on, not even bothering to look around.

'Don't leave me!' shouted Dana to the shadowy figure. 'Wait a minute!'

Liski Lup's voice suddenly sounded in her ear. 'Hop chop,' it was saying, 'I just can't stop. When there's work I never drop.'

I'd like to hop chop you, thought Dana. Here she was, light-years from home, with no idea of what was going on except that she was being chased by pirates and looking for lizards, tired and hungry with sand in her clothes and a cello in her arms, and all Liski Lup could say to her was, 'Hop chop'. It would

33

serve Liski right if Dana just stayed right here. Let her complete her mission without Dana if this was the way she was going to be. Even Mrs Preski would have been more sympathetic than this.

Fresh waves of sand rose up around her; the shadowy figure grew more shadowy.

On the other hand, if she stayed right here, soon both she and the cello would be part of the sand dune. Dana doubted that that would upset Liski either. With a resigned sigh, she struggled to her feet.

'I don't care what Mrs Preski or Liski Lup think about dragging a cello,' she muttered. 'I'm not carrying this dumb thing one more step.' She would have been perfectly happy to leave it right there in the middle of nowhere, but she did care what her mother would say if she came home without it. Trying not to inhale too much sand, Dana took a deep breath, bent her head against the wind and started to try walking again, pulling the cello behind her.

Liski Lup came to a sudden stop.

Dana, who hadn't realized she was there, ploughed into her. 'Do watch where you're going, Dana Bindle,' Liski scolded. 'We're not taking a stroll along a beach here you know.' She picked up her hat and gave it a shake. She gave Dana a look. It was similar to the look Dana's father had given her when she lost his favourite golf club.

'There are a few things you'll have to know if you want to be an apprentice Intergalactic Trouble Shooter,' Liski Lup said sniffily.

'But I don't—'

'And one of them is not walking into others. You never know what you might bump into.' Liski readjusted her goggles. 'And another is not to drag your cello through the sand, Dana Bindle. We're going to need it, you know. A great deal of my plan depends on it.'

Dana stared at Liski Lup. They were going to *need* her cello? What use was a cello on Wadric-5?

'But I don't know,' said Dana. 'I don't know anything about any plan. You still haven't told me what's happening.'

Liski Lup looked bemused. She cocked her head to one side. 'Haven't I?' she asked.

'No,' said Dana firmly and a little indignantly. 'No, you haven't.'

'Then I suppose I'd better,' said Liski. She dropped to the sand. 'We'll be there soon. And the tryouts are tomorrow morning, of course. I can't be stopping every nanosecond to explain things to you.'

'Be where?' asked Dana. 'What tryouts?'

Liski groaned. 'Has anyone ever told you that you're much too impatient? Not to mention illogical.' She eyed Dana critically. 'Why start in the middle when you can start at the start?'

Dana groaned. 'If you could just start *somewhere* . . .'

Liski Lup held her cape over her head and spread it open. 'Sit down in here and be quiet,' she ordered. 'I can't have you interrupting me with silly questions all the time.'

Dana was about to argue that her questions weren't silly, but then she thought better of it. What was the use? Liski Lup didn't listen to her any more than Iris Preski did. Dana and her cello sat across from Liski Lup. The cape closed around them like a tent.

'Now, if it's all the same to you, Dana Bindle,' said Liski Lup, 'I'll start at the beginning.'

Once upon a time, Liski Lup told Dana Bindle, the planet of Wadric-5 had been beautiful and nearly perfect. Everything was balanced and worked. You couldn't see the air. The desert took up only a fraction of the land mass and its sand was warm and dry. Wadric-5 had mountains and rivers, lakes and streams. It had lush tropical forests and dark, deep woods. Its vegetation took your breath away. Its creatures were remarkable and largely friendly. It didn't have papaya or carrots, that was true, but it had other things that were just as nice. Visitors used to come from every galaxy just to watch the three sunsets and the scarlet papamanga birds crowd the sky at dawn.

'Of course, the suns weren't lilac then, they were magenta,' said Liski. 'It does make a difference.'

'I can't see how—'

Liski Lup cut her off. 'Wadric-5 supported a great deal of life,' she continued pointedly. 'And most of it was reasonably intelligent. And very content.'

Dana brushed some sand from her mouth. 'What happened?'

'If you wouldn't interrupt me, I might be able to tell you,' said Liski.

Pardon me, thought Dana.

It was the same old thing, Liski Lup told her. Not all of the life Wadric-5 supported was intelligent, or content. Even most of the humanoid Wadrickians were sensible, but there was one breed of Wadrickian that had always been tricky customers.

'Too big for their quanta boots, if you ask me,' said

Liski. 'They never could leave anything alone. They always had to interfere. Instead of just speeding along from day to day like the rest of the universe, they wanted to control things.' Her eyes shone darkly. 'They got greedy.' She shrugged. 'Not that that matters, of course. The universe allows for a certain amount of stupidity and greed, as long as it's random and unorganized. It keeps things flowing.'

This time, Dana didn't ask what had happened.

Liski told her. 'What went wrong here was that the tricky Wadrickians found a leader. Someone whose greed and ambition were limitless. Someone who wanted control. Someone with plans.' She paused dramatically. 'The treacherous Maldox the Merciless!'

Under Maldox's leadership, the greedy Wadrickians got so greedy that, slowly but surely, they began to take over. They built hotels so high no one could see the sunset. They killed off the papamango birds to make capes of their feathers. They chopped down too many forests. They dried up too many rivers. They threw garbage into their oceans.

'That's why the water's that peculiar green,' Liski explained.

'Water?' echoed Dana. And then she remembered the green gunge spreading over the windscreen of the bus. 'You mean that really was water?'

'Not everywhere, of course,' said Liski. 'But here it is.'

Eventually, anyone with a gluon of sense who could leave Wadric-5 did just that.

'Except for the Wadrickians who were running things, of course,' said Liski. 'There were still quite a few things on Wadric-5 to make a profit from. And they realized, too, just how useful a large, unhospitable, abandoned planet could be. Especially since there was enough jungle and forest left to hide them and their loot.'

'Their loot?'

Liski nodded. 'Most of the remaining Wadrickians became pirates. They'd used up nearly all the resources of this planet, you see, but there were still millions of planets in the galaxies just waiting to be plundered. With Wadric-5 as their base, they could go anywhere, take anything, and never get caught.'

'What about the urds?' asked Dana. 'Where do they come in?' For once, Liski Lup didn't snap her head off for asking a question.

'Ah . . .' she sighed. 'The urds. The urds have always been here. And now they're almost extinct. The pirates sell their skins around the cosmos. Urd handbags are very much in demand in certain solar systems. The Stumbacci of Suma, for instance, pay a fortune for them.'

'Really?' It seemed impossible to Dana that anyone would want to keep their wallets and keys in anything as unattractive as an urd.

Liski nodded. 'I can see that you're as shocked and horrified by that as I am. Handbags. One of the most gentle, positive creatures in the cosmos, turned into something with a zip compartment and a strap.' She sighed again. 'It's very similar to the situation that made Culvert Cuvier, the greatest Intergalactic Trouble Shooter of them all, decide to free the dinosaurs from Earth.'

'Excuse me?' said Dana, missing the turn of the conversation. 'Who freed the dinosaurs?'

'Culvert Cuvier, Intergalactic Trouble Shooter, Grade Z,' said Liski Lup. 'It was a matter of life and death, as I'm sure you understand. If they'd hung around your planet, eventually they would have ended up as trunks and suitcases.'

Dana decided it was time to stick up for the Earth again. 'On *my* planet there are laws about killing endangered species,' said Dana coolly. 'Why don't they do that here? Why don't the police just stop the urds from being hunted?' This sounded to Dana like a reasonable question.

It didn't sound like a reasonable question to Liski Lup.

'Police? What police, Dana Bindle? The police don't come here. No one comes here except pirates, outlaws and intergalactic mercenaries.'

Dana frowned. 'I thought you said Wadric-5 was better than Earth.'

Liski shrugged. 'I exaggerated a little.'

Another thought occurred to Dana. It was almost as unpleasant as the one about her mother being from another planet. 'What do you mean no one comes here but pirates, outlaws and intergalactic mercenaries?' she asked. '*We're* here.'

'Of course *we're* here,' said Liski Lup. She suddenly pulled back her cape and stood up. 'We're on a mission. The very last shipment of urds is about to leave Wadric-5. When they go, everything that's left of the old Wadric-5 will go, too. The baloofa bugs will take over because there won't be anything around to eat them. They'll destroy the little jungle that remains. When the jungle's gone, all of Wadric-5 will be nothing but grey sand. And then, of course, the pirates will have to go somewhere else. Find another planet to destroy.' She pointed a finger at Dana. At some point when Dana wasn't paying attention, Liski had exchanged her gardening gloves for white cotton ones. 'That's why you and I are here: to make sure that the urds don't reach their destination.'

Dana got slowly to her feet. There were so many things that didn't quite make sense that she wasn't sure what question to ask next. She chose one at random. 'But what can I do?' she asked. 'I'm only a child.'

'And a human one at that,' said Liski Lup ungraciously. 'And one who never pays attention.' She started picking up her bags.

Dana leaned on her cello in a thoughtful way. 'But what about the pirates? If we set the urds free, won't they just catch them again?'

'Not if there aren't any pirates,' said Liski. She straightened her hat. 'Didn't I tell you? That's the first part of our mission. To get Maldox the Merciless and his thugs off Wadric-5 and into a black hole where they won't bother anyone for a while. Then we put the urds back in their jungle and normal life can begin again before it's too late.'

Dana might have wondered what Liski Lup considered 'normal life', or even how they were going to get the pirates into a black hole, but she was too busy wondering about Maldox the Merciless. She wasn't sure she liked the sound of him.

Dana remained motionless as Liski Lup moved forward again. 'And how are we going to do that?' she called after her.

'I haven't quite worked that out yet,' said Liski, beginning to glide. 'But I'm sure it'll come to me. Things usually do.'

Dana grabbed hold of her cello and started after Liski. 'What about the bus?' she called. 'When does the bus come back?'

'Twenty years,' Liski shouted over her shoulder. 'Give or take a week or two.'

CHAPTER FIVE

Welcome to Copenhagan

'Well? What do you think of that?' asked Liski Lup. She was lying on her stomach, squinting through the swirling sand.

Dana was lying beside her, also on her stomach and also squinting through the swirling sand. She almost felt as though she were in a cowboy film. Only instead of looking over a canyon at a wagon train, she was looking over a sand dune at three violet crescents vanishing behind trees taller than the tower blocks of home.

'It's a jungle,' said Dana.

'Of course it's a jungle,' said Liski. 'What did I tell you it was, a park?'

'But it's huge!'

After the story she'd been told about the destruction of Wadric-5, Dana had somehow expected the jungle to be smaller. More like a park, in fact.

'Ginormous,' agreed Liski. 'But nothing compared to what it used to be.' She removed a small silver box from her pocket and pointed it towards the jungle. She fiddled with its knobs. 'Due west,' she said at last. 'That's where we'll find them.'

'The urds?' asked Dana. She fervently hoped that she wasn't going to have to actually touch an urd in order to set them free. She really didn't feel comfortable with reptiles.

'Oh, no, not the urds,' said Liski. 'Though, of

course, they'll be there, too. No, I meant Maldox and his thugs.'

Dana wished Liski wouldn't keep calling them 'thugs'. It sounded much less romantic than 'pirates'.

Liski Lup pointed across Dana to the left. 'Do you see that narrow trail over there?' she asked.

Dana peered a little harder. Liski Lup was right, there was a narrow trail to the left that disappeared into the dense foliage of Wadric-5's jungle. Dana shook her head.

'It's not a trail, it's guests,' said Liski. 'Guests and entertainers for the party.'

Dana rubbed her eyes. She still only saw a narrow trail.

'Party?' asked Dana. 'What party?'

'Maldox the Merciless's birthday party, of course,' said Liski. 'It's the biggest event on Waldric-5. Which is logical, of course, since it's meant to be the last one as well. Everyone will be there.'

Not for the first time, Dana wished that Liski Lup would make sense. 'But I thought you said nobody would come to this planet,' said Dana. 'I thought you said it was too dangerous.'

'*Don't be a drain, use your brain*,' answered Liski. 'When I said *everybody*, I meant everybody no one else would invite to an exploding star.'

'Oh,' said Dana. 'Everybody.'

'And you and I, of course,' added Liski.

Dana looked at Liski Lup as that golf-club feeling came over her again. 'You and I?'

Liski had got a small telescope from somewhere and was watching the narrow trail through it. 'Oh, not as guests, Dana Bindle, don't worry. You won't have to dance the collapsing wave with the pirates. No one would expect you to do that. We'll be with the band.' She glanced quickly at Dana. 'And don't ask *what band*?' she ordered.

Dana bit her lip. It didn't seem to her that paying any amount of attention to Liski Lup made any difference. She still didn't know what was going on.

'That's why we want to get to the town tonight,' Liski went on. 'We'll need our rest if we're going to make the tryouts in the morning.'

Concentrate, Dana told herself. *Concentrate*. 'The tryouts for the band?' she guessed.

'Exactly.' Liski smiled. 'You see how easy it is when you listen?'

'But, Ms Lup,' said Dana, 'I can't try out for a band. Mrs Preski says I'm not even ready to join the junior orchestra. Mrs Preski says I have no flow.'

'*Flow, blow*,' sang Liski Lup. '*Never stop when others go.*' She smiled again. 'It's a good thing Mrs Preski isn't one of the judges, isn't it?' she asked. 'You see how things have a way of working out?'

Dana didn't see that things were working out at all, but she decided it might be better not to say so. Instead, she made a different mistake. 'But surely if the pirates knew we were on the bus they'll be waiting for us?' she said.

Liski Lup was getting to her feet again. 'What makes you think they knew we were on the bus?' she asked, brushing sand from her cape.

She couldn't be accused of inattention this time. 'Because they attacked us,' said Dana.

The Intergalactic Trouble Shooter, Grade Z, picked up her things. 'Oh, they weren't attacking us,' she said breezily. 'Not *personally*. They were just buzzing the bus for fun.'

'You mean they didn't know we were on it?'

'Oh, no. They knew we *weren't* on it.' She started over the ridge of the sand dune. 'No one with a gluon of sense would come to Wadric-5 by bus. Not and get off.'

Dana was still considering the full significance of this when Liski Lup stopped and turned around. She held up three fingers. 'And the third and most important rule, Dana Bindle,' she said solemnly, 'is not to let the pirates know that you're human.' She adjusted her goggles. 'They really don't care for humans.'

Well, there was a cheery bit of news. 'But won't they know I'm human?' asked Dana.

'Not if you don't tell them,' said Liski. 'If you do as I say, they'll think you're a sensible Wadrickian, just visiting, like me.' She disappeared over the rise in a cloud of sand.

Dana was sitting by herself in a room of the Copenhagan Guest House. It was a small, dark bare room, and Dana was eating a banana while she listened nervously to what seemed to be very large creatures stampeding through the hallway.

Something started thumping on the ceiling. The room began to shake.

Dana looked up. Unlike the ceiling of her bedroom at home, which was hard and smooth, the ceiling of room twenty-four was bumpy and bulging. Not only was it bumpy and bulging, but the bumps and bulges were moving. She could make out knees, feet, hands, elbows, bums and shoulders pressing into the floor above her, as though it were made of canvas. The guests upstairs must be having a fight.

Dana threw down her banana. No matter how hungry she was, she couldn't concentrate on food when the room was shaking and the ceiling was moving like that. Where on Wadric-5 was Liski Lup? Why didn't she come back?

Something started bellowing in the hall. If Dana had been back on Earth, Dana would have thought that it must be an elephant. On Wadric-5, she wasn't so sure. If the glimpse of the inhabitants of the town of Copenhagan she'd had as she followed Liski Lup to the guest house was a guide to go by, it could be anything.

Dana sighed unhappily. 'I don't like this,' she announced to the empty room. 'I really don't. I'd rather be having a cello lesson.'

She wrapped her cape around her a little more snugly, trying to get less cold. She shifted her position, trying to get less uncomfortable.

'Don't think about the howling,' she told herself. 'It's probably nothing. It's probably the way they greet each other here.' She picked up her banana again. 'And don't look at the ceiling. They're probably not really fighting. They're probably just fooling around.'

Dana once stayed in a guest house in Cornwall with her parents, and that was very warm and comfortable. It had furniture and central heating. It had beds. Wadrickian guest houses, however, did not have beds, or any other sort of furniture. There

46

wasn't even a lamp. There was only one small, dirty window, shaped like a hole that had been punched in the wall. It looked out at the crumbling building across the way. Pulsating coloured lights showed through it and noise from the street drifted into the room. It was not the noise that drifted into the Bindle's living room from Hollyrod Drive. There was a lot of shouting, bleeping, clanging, fizzing, whooping and rough laughter. The only sound that reminded Dana of Hollyrod Drive was a shrill persistant wail she took to be car alarms.

Dana sighed. She looked at her watch again. It was blue and had yellow fishes swimming between the numbers. Her parents had given it to her for her birthday. It wasn't working. Its hands had stopped at five forty-five.

'I thought she said she was coming right back,' Dana grumbled to herself.

Which was true. The last thing Liski Lup said to her was, 'You wait here, Dana Bindle, and mind our things. It's been a long while since I've been to Copenhagan. I want to have a look around. I'll be right back.'

But that was a long time ago.

The thumping overhead got louder. Ignoring her own warning, Dana looked up just as a foot came through the ceiling. It was a large, toeless foot the colour of lemon jelly. Dana screamed.

'Can't I leave you alone for a nanosecond without you making a commotion?'

Dana stopped screaming. Liski Lup was standing in the doorway, holding what looked like an over-sized red trumpet in her hands. She seemed cross.

47

'B – b – but—' stammered Dana, pointing to the ceiling. 'The foot!'

Liski Lup scowled at the dangling foot. 'Wrestling practice,' said Liski. She dropped the trumpet to the floor. 'I've never cared for wrestling.'

'Hold still, Dana Bindle. You're as jumpy as an electron.'

'I can't help it,' grumbled Dana. 'You're hurting me.'

It was morning. A fragile lilac light was coming through the window. The Copenhagan Guest House was eerily quiet. The ceiling had stopped bulging. The foot was gone. Dana's cello and Liski Lup's over-sized red trumpet were ready by the door. Liski Lup was helping Dana get ready for the auditions.

'*Who cares about pain when there's so much to gain?*' boomed Liski. She was in a very good mood.

Dana, however, was not in a good mood, very or otherwise. She was nervous. She didn't want to try out for the birthday band. The only music she had with her was *Learning the Cello – Book Four*, not that that mattered. She wouldn't be able to play anything anyway. After a night on Wadric-5, she wasn't even sure that she could tune the cello without help. She would never be able to concentrate on sitting right and keeping her elbow in the correct position and flowing.

'There!' Liski Lup stepped back, admiring her handiwork. 'The eyes are a problem, of course. If anyone asks why they're that peculiar blue just tell them you got caught in a hyperdimension.' She smiled without modesty. 'But on the whole, I'd say that not even your own mother would guess you weren't really a sensible Wadrickian now.'

She held her palm up in front of Dana so that Dana could see herself in the miniature television screen.

Dana stared at her image. Like Liski Lup, Dana was wearing baggy floral shorts, a white T-shirt that had the words I WAS ON WADRIC-5 FOR MALDOX'S 411TH BIRTHDAY printed on its front, and multi-coloured quanta boots. Dana's straight brown hair had been twisted into dozens of tiny plaits with tiny silver moons on the ends. If Dana's mother were to see her like this, she wouldn't think she was a sensible Wadrickian. She'd think she'd lost her mind.

'But what if I fail the tryouts?' asked Dana. 'What if I don't make the band?'

'Of course you'll make the band,' said Liski. 'You have to make the band. If you don't make the band, we won't get into pirate headquarters.'

'Yes, but—'

'And if we don't get into pirate headquarters, we won't be able to stow away on the ship carrying the last shipment of urds to Suma.'

'Yes, but—'

'And if we don't stow away on the ship, we won't be able to lose the pirates in the nearest black hole and return the urds to their natural habitat.'

'Yes, but what if I *don't* make the band?'

'Humans!' Liski Lup dropped her hand. 'Why do you worry about every little thing, Dana Bindle? Why don't you just go with the flow?'

Which was what Mrs Preski was always telling her, more or less. 'That's the trouble,' said Dana. 'I can't go with the flow. I have too much trouble trying to read the music.'

Liski Lupp picked up her trumpet. 'Read the music? Is that what's worrying you? That you won't be able to read the music?' She opened the door and stepped into the hall.

Dana picked up her cello. 'Yes,' she said, following the sensible Wadrickian down the stairs. 'Yes, it is. Mrs Preski says—'

'Well, you don't have to worry about that,' said Liski Lup. 'No one reads music here. We don't believe in it. We believe in improvisation.'

Dana bumped into Liski as she stopped in front of a door marked Leave.

'Improvisation?' asked Dana.

'Of course,' said Ms Lup. 'It's the way of the cosmos, isn't it?'

Dana frowned. It might be the way of the cosmos, but it certainly wasn't the way of *Learning the Cello – Book Four* or of Mrs Preski.

'But I don't think—' began Dana.

Liski cut her off. 'I know you don't,' she said. 'Which would be an advantage if you just wouldn't talk so much as well.' She took a pencil from her pocket. It was black and covered with silver stars that shone like prisms. 'Are you ready for this, Dana Bindle?' she asked. 'You are about to see Copenhagan in daylight.' She pointed the pencil at the door. The door opened.

Dana stepped into the hot, humid morning beside Liski Lup. The streets of the town were deserted and most of the buildings were in need of repair. Rubbish was piled up in the gutters. The road was unpaved and rutted. Everything stank.

Suddenly the morning was filled with shrill wails.

Dana put her hands to her ears. 'It's those car alarms, again,' she said. 'But I don't see any cars.'

'Those aren't car alarms,' said Liski, as the wailing got closer and more insistent. 'Those are solid maser-lasers.'

'They're *what*?'

'Guns, to you,' said Liski Lup. 'But don't worry, they're just firing randomly, they're not aiming at us.' She threw herself to the ground. 'Duck!'

Dana and her cello crouched down beside Liski Lup as several deep red beams flashed over their heads.

'Welcome to Copenhagan,' said Liski Lup. 'My home town.'

CHAPTER SIX

I'll Survive Maldox the Merciless's 411th Birthday. Will You?

The auditions to be part of the band at Maldox the Merciless's birthday party were being held in an old warehouse down by the river.

Ducking and weaving between the colourful random firing of solid maser-lasers, Liski Lup led Dana across the centre of Copenhagan to the docks. On the way, Liski gave Dana a guided tour of Copenhagan. She pointed out the building where she first went to school. She pointed out the field where she crashed her first solo-shuttle. She pointed out the shop where she used to buy imported carrots. They came to the river. 'And that,' she said, indicating a spot on the opposite bank, 'is where I used to watch the papamangos rise at dawn.'

The building where Liski first went to school was now a gambling parlour. The field was grey sand. The shop was a bar. The river was burning.

'That can't be the river,' said Dana. 'It's on fire. Water can't burn.'

'Wadrickian ingenuity,' said Liski. She continued on to the warehouse. 'The only other planet that happens on is Earth.'

Dana followed Liski inside. 'Are you sure we're in

the right place?' she whispered, pulling her cello closer.

'Of course I'm sure this is the right place.' The golden eyes snapped. 'What other place could it be?'

The wrong place, thought Dana.

Dana and Liski Lup were standing in the entrance of an old warehouse down by the river. To one side was the queue for obtaining your audition number. The auditions themselves were being held at the front, where several musicians seemed to be trying out at once. At least Dana assumed they were musicians, they were all holding instruments. But they weren't anything like the members of Mrs Preski's chamber music quartet. The room was incredibly noisy and crowded. Dana just wished it were noisy with the normal sounds of conversation and laughter and not the beeps, squeaks, howls, moans and intermittant hummings that passed for verbal communication on Wadric-5. She wished that it were crowded with people.

'They don't look like musicians,' said Dana.

'Don't they?' said Liski Lup. She grabbed Dana's arm and started pulling her through the mob.

'No,' said Dana. 'No, they don't.' Musicians were serious and intense. They were quiet and respectable-looking. They wore suits.

'Humans rely too much on appearances,' said Liski Lup shortly. She steered Dana to the left. 'What do they look like, Dana Bindle, if they don't look like musicians?'

That was a difficult question to answer. Dana glanced around her. There were metallic robots with flashing lights. There were stiff, sober-faced androids. There were humanoids of every size, texture, colour and ear shape. There were monstrous creatures with extra eyes, heads, arms, sensors and ears. There were monstrous creatures with the correct number of parts. No one was wearing a suit. Except for the rather large trombonist in the red swimming trunks, who looked like an iguana, and the small figure all in black with a sheet of dark Perspex where his face should have been, who looked like a motorcycle courier, none of the creatures waiting for the auditions for the birthday band looked very much like anything Dana had ever seen before.

'*Things*,' said Dana. 'They look like *things*.'

Liski Lup shoved her on the queue. 'And what do you think you look like to *them*?' she asked.

Now there was a question. Dana could only hope that the answer wasn't 'Supper.'

Dana reckoned that the humanoid sitting at the computer on the luminous rock facing the queue, handing out the audition numbers, must be a Wadrickian pirate. There was something about him. Dana wasn't sure if it was the very large maser-laser strapped across his back, or because his hair, though clumped and filthy, was done in dozens of plaits, each tipped with a tiny ebony skull.

'One of the worst,' affirmed Liski Lup. 'That's Cayman the Cruel, Maldox's cousin.'

'Cayman the Cruel?' Dana moved ahead with the bear-like creature in the jewelled jumpsuit in front of her.

Liski followed. 'He has what you might call a difficult personality,' said Liski. 'Whatever you do, don't attract his attention. My advice is to get your number as quickly as possible and get out of his visual range. In Cayman the Cruel's case, that old Mungolfian proverb, *The less you say, the less you have to regret later*, applies to bones, not feelings.'

'Thanks for the advice,' said Dana. She had finally found something to take her mind off failing the tryouts: not surviving to fail the tryouts.

Liski slipped something into her hand. 'Here,' she said, 'you'll need these.'

Dana glanced at her palm. In it were two small, round objects that looked rather like miniature tea-balls. 'What are they?'

'They're intergalactic audio-transformers,' said Liski. 'Slip one into your ear and one into your mouth, and you'll be able to understand what's being said, and they'll be able to understand you.' She gave Dana a look. 'Just try to pay attention, Dana Bindle. Just this once.'

Dana paid attention. Half-hidden behind her cello, she listened as the other hopefuls stepped up in turn to get their audition numbers. Cayman, glaring into his computer, asked each of them two questions, then handed over a metal disc.

Just do exactly what they do, Dana kept telling herself. *Cayman asks you your name, and you tell him. Cayman asks you what instrument you play, and you tell him. Cayman gives you a number and you go and wait for it to be called.*

The bear-like creature in the jewelled jumpsuit took its disc and moved away. Liski Lup poked Dana with her trumpet. *'Don't be slow, just go go go . . .'* she hissed.

Dana went.

Up close, Cayman the Cruel was a lot more unpleasant looking than he was from a distance through a mob of extra-terrestrials. His skin was the colour of the Wadrickian sky, and crossed with scars in every hue of the spectrum. She couldn't see his eyes because of the way he was sitting, but his lips were as thin as string. It seemed unlikely to Dana that he'd ever used them to smile. He was dressed all in yellow. His T-shirt read: I WILL SURVIVE MALDOX'S 411TH BIRTHDAY PARTY. WILL YOU? Altogether, the effect was a little unsettling.

'Name?' growled Cayman.

'Dana Bindle,' Dana promptly answered.

He tapped out her name on the keyboard. 'Instrument?'

'Cello,' said Dana.

Cayman the Cruel did not type 'cello' into the computer. He did not hand her a disc with her number on it. He looked up. She had caught his attention. Dana's heart sank like a golf club tied around a concrete pillar and tossed into a very deep lake.

'What?' His eyes weren't gold like Liski Lup's, but a purple so dark it was almost black.

'Cello,' Dana repeated.

'What?'

'Cello.'

He pointed. 'Is that your cello?'

Dana nodded. She held it up. 'Yes,' she said. 'Yes, this is my cello.'

56

He leaned forward on his computer. 'That's not a cello,' he said.

Dana had been wrong. Cayman the Cruel did smile. Though not in such a way that you would be likely to ask him to do it again.

'That's a Beda-X Dematerializer.'

'No, it's not,' said Dana politely but firmly. 'It's a cello.'

Cayman the Cruel didn't like being corrected any more than Liski Lup did. 'Are you saying that I don't know a Beda-X Dematerializer when I see one?' he roared.

Dana wished she knew what she was saying. 'Oh, no, no,' she answered quickly. 'I'm just saying that this is a cello.'

He stood up. He was not a small pirate. 'And I'm saying it's a Beda-X Dematerializer.'

'Tell him,' hissed Dana, turning behind her to Liski Lup. 'Tell him it just looks like a Beda-X Dematerializer.' Behind her was a robot the shape of a beehive and the red of a post box. It was holding a clarinet. Liski Lup was nowhere in sight.

Cayman the Cruel banged on his rock. 'Look at me when I'm talking to you!' he ordered.

Dana looked.

'What are you doing trying to sneak in here with a Beda-X Dematerializer?' he demanded. 'You're not by any chance an Intergalactic Trouble Shooter, are you?'

For the first time since she followed Liski Lup into the bus, Dana wished she were an Intergalactic Trouble Shooter. Then she might know what to do.

At least Mrs Preski wasn't here to contradict her.

'I'm a cello player,' said Dana. 'Look,' she went on, hastily undoing the case, 'this is my cello.'

'Play it,' said Caymen the Cruel.

'Excuse me?' Golf clubs were sinking into lakes in Dana's stomach at a rate of thousands, perhaps even millions.

'Play it!' He clapped his hand four times. The room went totally silent. 'Dana Bindle is going to play the cello for us!' shouted Cayman.

Dana could see herself in the dark purple sheen of the pirate's eyes. She looked very small.

'Decide what you're going to play for us on your cello, Dana Bindle,' said Cayman the Cruel. 'Now.'

It was an easy choice to make. There was only one tune that Dana knew all the way through.

Aware that everyone was watching her, Dana picked up her bow. She took a deep breath. She closed her eyes. *Please*, she begged silently. *Please don't let me be off-key.*

Slowly and unsurely, the strains of 'Twinkle, Twinkle, Little Star' began to fill the warehouse. It was off-key. And it wasn't a rendition that flowed, as Mrs Preski would have quickly pointed out, but much to Dana's relief it was recognizable.

Cayman the Cruel recognized it. 'That's "Implode, Implode, Dying Star"!' he shouted. 'I've never met anyone who could play it before.'

Dana continued to scrape the bow across the strings, wondering if this was good news or bad news.

It was both.

Cayman the Cruel leapt over his glowing computer and his glowing rock. He grabbed her by the shoulders. 'That's Maldox's favourite song!' he cried. 'His mother used to sing it to him when he was a child. He hasn't heard it for at least two hundred years.'

'Oh, what a shame,' said Dana.

Cayman the Cruel thought it was a shame, too. 'But tonight he shall hear it!' he announced. 'Tonight Dana Bindle will play "Implode, Implode, Dying Star" when we bring out the cake.'

Dana stopped breathing. *I will?*

'Only you'll have to sit with the guitars,' said Cayman. 'You're the only cello in the band.'

CHAPTER SEVEN

Happy Birthday to You, Happy Birthday to You, Happy Birthday, Dear Maldox, Happy Birthday to You

'But it wasn't my fault,' whispered Dana.

She and Liski Lup were in the musicians' changing room, getting ready for the party. Getting ready for the party meant putting on the neon-orange cummerbund and hot-pink jacket with electric trim that was the band members' uniform. The other thirty-six members of the birthday band were also in the changing room getting ready for the party, however, so Dana was trying not to speak too loudly. Both the heads of the guitar player tuning up on their left had been giving her suspicious looks.

'Wasn't it?' asked Liski Lup. She tied a glittering scarf around her head like a turban and appraised herself in the palm of her hand. She liked what she saw. 'And whose fault was it, if it isn't yours? *Mine*?' She closed her hand.

It was clear from the tone of Ms Lup's voice that she considered that a preposterous idea. Dana, however, did not consider it at all preposterous. It seemed to Dana that if it was anyone's fault that Cayman the Cruel had singled her out and forced her to play 'Twinkle, Twinkle, Little Star' in front of the entire audition hall, it was the fault of Liski Lup, Intergalactic Trouble Shooter, Grade Z, not Dana Bindle, beginner cellist, level four.

'But you abandoned me!' Dana squealed. She jumped as something dank and knobbly brushed against her arm. A flautist bearing a striking resemblance to the mini-dinosaur *Heterodontosaurus tucki* was pushing past her. 'I turned around and you were gone.'

'I wasn't *gone*,' said Liski coolly. 'I simply wasn't there. Those are two totally different conditions.' She gave a Mrs Iris Preski-like sniff. 'One of us had to keep her anonymity,' she added pointedly.

Dana pulled her cello out of the way of the enormous webbed orange feet of a passing saxophonist. 'But—'

'But my busted superconductor,' snapped Liski. 'I told you not to bring attention to yourself, and what did you do? You brought attention to yourself. You couldn't have brought more attention to yourself if you'd been wearing a baseball cap and waving an electron banner that said I COME FROM EARTH.'

'That's not fair!' Dana's voice squeaked with indignation. 'What else could I do?'

'Do?' echoed Liski Lup. 'What else could you *do*?' She spread out her arms, hitting something with golden skin as smooth as a boiled egg and a banjo strapped across its chest. Green and purple sparks showered down on them. Liski Lup didn't notice; or, if she noticed, didn't care. 'There is nothing in the universe but possibilities, and you couldn't think of anything else to *do* except play "Implode, Implode, Dying Star"?' She picked up her trumpet. 'You could have played some ragtime, Dana Bindle. You could have played some blues. You could have played any old standard like "You're the Only Gurgletroyd for Me". You didn't have to play Maldox the Merciless's favourite song and get yourself a solo tonight.'

Liski Lup was even less pleased about Dana's solo than Dana was. Liski Lup said that now *everyone* had noticed Dana it was going to be hard for them to sneak off and stow away on the ship while the party was at its height; if not impossible.

'Maybe Cayman the Cruel will forget about the song,' said Dana. 'You know, in the excitement of the celebration and everything . . .'

'Forget?' Liski Lup pointed her trumpet at Dana. 'Cayman the Cruel remembers the first time he ever picked a bone out of his fangs. He's not going to forget your—'

She broke off as a sudden burst of gunfire sounded over their heads.

Feeling that she was beginning to get the knack of life on Wadric-5, Dana and her cello hit the ground.

'*Now* what do you think you're doing, Dana Bindle?'

Cautiously, Dana raised her head. Liski Lup was staring down at her with her mouth all screwed up in what in a piece of string would have been a knot. 'I'm getting out of shooting range,' she explained.

It really was amazing how much Liski Lup could remind her of Mrs Preski. Like now, for instance.

'That was last call, not an armed attack,' said Liski flatly. 'The party's about to begin.'

Dana looked around. It was true, everything else was leaving the room through the wall without the door.

Liski started after them. 'Just a few more words of advice, Dana Bindle,' said Liski as Dana scrambled to her feet. 'Don't leave your seat. Don't do an encore. Don't speak. And whatever you do, don't lose sight of me or you'll miss my signal. Do you think you can do those few simple things?'

Dana stopped to dust off her cello. 'Of course I can,' said Dana. When she looked up Liski Lup was gone.

This isn't anything like my *last birthday party*, thought Dana as she lugged her cello to the stage in the centre of the room.

Dana's last birthday party had been held at the local pizza restaurant. They'd been given a table by the window, where they could look out at the passers-by and the traffic, and the passers-by and the traffic could look in at them.

Maldox the Merciless's 411th birthday party, on the other hand, was being held in a glass pod on top of the highest building in Copenhagan. Surrounding them like an inverted bowl were trillions of stars and gaseous masses. Down to the west Dana could make out the lush, steamy remains of the rainforest; to the east were the charred remains of the rest of the planet; moored to the top of the pod was the gleaming white pirates' ship, ready to take its last load of urds to the big factory on Suma.

For Dana's last birthday party, the manager of Pizza Pizzaz had let Dana's mother tape a few balloons and a sign that said HAPPY BIRTHDAY DANA to one wall of the restaurant.

The room where Maldox's party was taking place, however, was decorated with so many pulsating coloured lights and floating luminiferous glass balls that it was almost blinding. Dana stumbled several times as she made her way across the room, and finally crashed into the stage, which floated above the floor on a platform clear as crystal.

'Oof!' cried Dana.

'Shake an appendage!' ordered a gruff voice above her. 'We're ready to start.'

Dana looked up. Sitting on a stool that hovered in the air was a guitar player with the head and skin of a fresh-water trout.

Something heavy crashed to the ground behind her. The pirates were getting restless They were shouting and yelling. They were popping balloons. They were knocking over chairs. They were throwing bits of food and wads of paper at each other. Several of the pirates were playing darts with laser beams, while another group had begun a burping contest.

Dana scrambled onto the stage. She heaved herself onto one of the hovering stools and scanned the horn section for Liski Lup. She could see a trumpet player with a furry green head, and a trombonist with an iridescent blue head, and a cornet player with a rather unfortunate snout with a harpoon through it, but no Integalactic Trouble Shooter, Grade Z.

One of the luminiferous balls exploded near Dana's left ear. She stopped looking for Liski. Another shattered at her feet.

'Someone's shooting at us!' shrieked Dana.

'Shut your oral cavity!' hissed the trout. 'No one's

shooting at us yet. Can't you see that's Maldox the Merciless himself? He always gets over-excited on occasions like this.'

Dana glanced warily to the front. Maldox the Merciless was a small, slender humanoid with copper skin and eyes that reminded Dana of chocolate digestives. Like the other pirates, he was smartly dressed in a blue and white pinstriped suit. His shirt was red and made of silk. On his head was a party hat trimmed with tinsel. Alizarin and ochre smoke poured from its top. The pirate leader was standing in the middle of an enormous table, beneath a canopy of glowing balls, waving a silver pea-shooter and screaming, 'Music! Music! It's time to dance!'

Dana ducked as another ball shattered behind her. Something sharp and hard kicked Dana's ankle. It was the trout. 'Quishel,' he whispered.

'What?' Dana whispered back.

'Quishel.' He jerked his head towards the rest of the band.

It was then that she realized that the music had begun.

Everyone was playing with what Mrs Preski would have called considerable 'flow'. Those who had toes were tapping them. Those who didn't have toes were tapping other things. Dana tried to concentrate. Another ball exploded over her head.

'Are you *sure* he's not shooting at us?' she whispered to the trout.

'Of course I am,' he whispered back. 'If Maldox were aiming at us he wouldn't miss.'

Dana was later to remember those words. They

didn't sound half as comforting then as they did right now.

Cayman the Cruel gently clapped his hands four times and the entire room went silent. All eyes, no matter what their shape, number or colour, turned to him.

'It's time for the cake!' he announced.

Reluctantly, Dana put down her bow. Playing with a band of extra-terrestrials was nothing like accompanying Mrs Iris Preski. Even though she'd begun by only pretending to play, as the night wore on she'd caught their liveliness and exuberance and started getting into the music. She improvised. She flowed. She had a good time.

Dana wiped her forehead with her pink sleeve. She was also exhausted. Wadrickian pirates and the friends of Wadrickian pirates were even more fond of dancing than they were of fighting, burping and throwing food at one another. Whenever the band tried to stop, Maldox started shooting luminiferous balls again and shouting for just one more song.

Six small melon-orange robots wheeled the cake into the pod. The cake was as big as the kitchen table back on Hollyrod Drive, and had so many flames blazing across its top that it reminded Dana of the time she was helping her father to get the barbecue going and her attention wandered for a second and she poured a whole tin of lighter fluid over the coals.

Cayman the Cruel put an affectionate, cousinly hand around the shoulder of Maldox the Merciless.

He smiled at Maldox, and Maldox smiled back at him. It wasn't a particularly pleasant sight, but if Dana's mother had been present, she would probably have taken their picture. Dana's mother had taken forty-eight pictures of people smiling at each other at Dana's birthday party, including several of people at other tables whom no one knew.

'And now,' said Cayman, 'for my special surprise.' He turned to the band. He was still smiling. He raised his hand. The stage went dark except for a single spot of white light. It took a few seconds for Dana to realize that the white light was shining on her. She'd been having such a good time that she'd forgotten about her solo entirely.

'Dana Bindle!' shouted Cayman the Cruel. 'Play!'

Dana gave another glance around the stage. Now, she felt, would be a really good time for Liski Lup to signal her to make their escape.

The trout gave her a prod with the neck of his guitar. 'Can't you understand Wadrickian?' he hissed. 'Play!'

Dana played. Slowly and hesitatingly at first, and then with more confidence and even a bit of flow as she realized the effect her song was having on Maldox the Merciless. There were tears in his eyes.

'Sing!' sobbed Maldox. 'Dana Bindle, sing!'

The guests took up the chant. 'Sing, Dana Bindle!' they shouted. 'Sing.'

Dana knew that in a universe made up of nothing but possibilities, there must be something else she could do besides sing, but as usual she couldn't think of what that something might be. She started to sing.

'Twinkle, twinkle, little star,' sang Dana, 'how I wonder what you are. Up above the world so high, like a diamond in the sky . . .'

The effect was instantaneous. The tears froze on Maldox's copper cheeks. Cayman the Cruel stopped smiling.

'That's not "Implode, Implode, Dying Star"!' screamed Cayman. 'You're not Wadrickian! You're human!'

'Seize it!' screamed Maldox.

Before Dana could even consider another possible course of action, like running, two strong, cold hands clasped her arms and lifted her and her cello into the air. She was still playing as she was hurried towards the exit. She was still playing when she saw Liski Lup, sitting in the horn section with her trumpet on her lap. Liski Lup was looking right at her. It was a Mrs Iris Preski sort of look.

CHAPTER EIGHT

There's More than One Way to Spin a Hadron

After Dana was hurried from the hall, the pirates carried her along the dark waterfront and out to the edge of the city, where their ship was waiting. They carried her into the ship and through the winding corridors till they reached what looked like a solid wall. The wall opened and they threw Dana in.

'Maldox will see to you later!' shouted one of the pirates as the wall began to close behind Dana.

The other pirates laughed.

Just in the nick of time, when Dana thought she would never see the Intergalactic Trouble Shooter, Grade Z, again, or much else come to that, Liski Lup reappeared. She dropped suddenly through the ceiling, still shaking the confetti from the party off her clothes.

Dana had been sitting on the floor, sulking and thinking over all the things she'd done since leaving Mrs Preski's on Thursday evening that she wished she hadn't. 'Where have you been?' she demanded, as soon as she saw Liski. 'Why did you disappear like that? I thought you'd forgotten all about me.'

Liski Lup dropped her bags. Shiny flakes of red and green and gold and silver drifted around her. She pulled out a cushion and sat down.

'Been?' repeated the Intergalactic Trouble Shooter. 'Where do you think I've been?' She flapped her arms. 'Here, there, and everywhere. Just like everything else.'

'But I thought you were meant to be looking out for me,' protested Dana crossly. 'I thought we were working together.'

Liski wasn't paying her so much as a gluon of attention. Instead, she was removing a very large and very gooey piece of birthday cake from one of her bags. 'It's a good thing for you that there's more than one way to spin a hadron,' Liski Lup commented, 'or you would have made a real mess of things this time.' She bit into the cake. 'But, of course, it's just as I always say. *Never fret and never pout, things have a way of working out.*'

'I don't see how this is things working out,' answered Dana. Dana was sitting in a bare room no larger than her wardrobe back home. Like her wardrobe, this room had no windows. Unlike her wardrobe, it had steel bars instead of a door. The steel bars hummed. Dana sounded fretful and looked pretty pouty.

'Don't you?' asked Liski. She seemed to find this surprising.

'No,' said Dana shortly. 'I don't. It seems to me that nothing's working out.' At least part of the reason Dana sounded fretful and looked pouty was because Liski Lup was not in the cell with her. She was on the other side of the humming steel bars. Eating birthday cake.

'Humans,' said Liski, sighing impatiently, 'you do have trouble taking the larger view.' She brushed some crumbs from her mouth. 'We're on Maldox the

70

Merciless's ship, aren't we?' she asked, as though this were the only important point. 'What's that, I'd like to know, if it isn't things working out?' She eyed Dana sourly. 'As far as I can see, everything's going according to plan.'

Not for the first time, Dana wondered if perhaps she should have paid more attention when Liski Lup was explaining her plan. There seemed to be a few significant details Dana hadn't been aware of. 'But I'm in jail,' wailed Dana. 'Don't tell me you planned for that!'

'Perhaps not exactly, but then it doesn't always matter how things happen, just that they do.' Liski licked icing from her fingers. 'I did plan for us to be on our way to a black hole, and we are that.' She seemed to think this was good news.

'But we're only going to the black hole to throw me in it,' Dana pointed out. As little as Dana knew about black holes, she was reasonably certain that they weren't the sort of places you went for a quick visit.

Liski Lup didn't seem too disturbed by the fact that the pirates were planning to leave Dana Bindle and her cello in a black hole.

'In, bin,' said Liski Lup brightly. '*If you don't lose sometimes, you never win.*' She removed another slice of cake and a small, thin black tube from her carriers. She put the tube on the floor. 'And anyway, whose fault is it that you're in jail? *Mine?*' she asked indignantly. 'Didn't I tell you not to let Maldox and his thugs know that you're human?' She nibbled at her cake. 'That's another trouble with you humans,' she

71

decided. 'The minute you're told *not* to do something, you go right ahead and do it as quickly as you can. It's one of your most obvious genetic flaws.'

Dana winced with pain as she tried to get her left leg into a more comfortable position. As far as she was concerned, one of the most obvious human genetic flaws was the inability to sit in a small, locked space without having your leg go to sleep.

'But I didn't,' Dana protested. 'I was trying not to give myself away, you know. I was doing my best.'

Liski Lup gave her a look. It was a critical look. 'Well, your best doesn't seem to be all that good, does it, Dana Bindle?' she asked. 'You might as well have worn a sign that said: I live on Hollyrod Drive and I like chips and sausage pizza.' She flicked some crumbs from her blouse. 'Imagine singing "Twinkle, Twinkle, Little Star" to Maldox the Merciless. It's like giving a chocolate bar to a Berba.'

Dana could tell that Liski was waiting for her to ask what happened when you gave a chocolate bar to a Berba – assuming, of course, that you weren't immediately hauled off and thrown into a cell in some dark corner of a spaceship hurtling towards a black hole – but she was getting pretty fed up with Liski Lup and her attitude, so she didn't.

This, however, didn't bother Liski Lup. She carried on as though Dana had asked.

'It blows up,' she answered. 'In the course of human history, more than one exploding Berba with chocolate on its breath has been mistaken for a bomb.' She smiled reassuringly. 'Let's look at the bright side, though, shall we?' she continued. 'If

Maldox hadn't known you were human the probabilities are that we wouldn't be here now. He would simply have tossed you into the jungle for being a mad musician and you would have sunk in the swamp.'

This news wasn't nearly as comforting as Liski made it sound. Because Maldox had known that no one but a human would know 'Twinkle, Twinkle, Little Star', he had taken her on board his ship to make her walk the plank in deepest space. Dana couldn't help wondering if sinking in a swamp wasn't infinitesimally preferable to falling through a black hole.

'I still don't see what "Twinkle, Twinkle, Little Star" has to do with it,' Dana grumbled. 'Maldox *told* me to sing that song. I couldn't say no, could I?'

'He told you no such thing,' snapped Liski. She brushed her hands on her neon-orange cummerbund. 'What he told you to sing was "Implode, Implode, Dying Star". Which you, of course, did not do. That's another of your unfortunate human traits; doing what no one wants you to do.'

Dana sighed. As far as she could see, an unfortunate Wadrickian trait was always thinking you were right. 'I don't see what difference it makes,' argued Dana. 'They're the same song.'

'Are they?' asked Liski.

Dana could tell that this was a trick question. Her expression became a little more fretful. They definitely *sounded* like the same song. 'I don't understand—'

'Well, that makes a change, doesn't it?' Liski

picked up the black tube and pointed it at Dana. 'I'd have thought that even *you* would have figured it out by now,' she said.

'Figured out what?'

The black tube waggled. 'I'll give you a clue,' said the ever-helpful Ms Lup. 'The birthday party is not a Wadrickian concept. Sensible Wadrickians celebrate their birthdays by going into a cosmic trance to get in touch with their inner selves, not by eating too much while wearing a paper hat.'

Dana was tempted to point out that the only one eating too much at the moment was the sensible Wadrickian, Ms Liski Lup, but she doubted that this would make the Intergalactic Trouble Shooter think any better of her. Instead, she frowned in concentration, trying to make sense of Liski's clue. 'Are you saying that Maldox the Merciless is *human*?' she asked at last.

'Half human,' said Liski. 'His father was from Devon.'

Dana's Aunt Julia lived in Devon. 'Devon?' Dana repeated. Dana's Aunt Julia grew roses and was nothing at all like Maldox the Merciless.

'Someone has to be from Devon, don't they?' Liski leaned her back against the wall of the ship. 'I don't know if Maldox's father was typical of men from Devon or not, but he proved a poor choice as far as Maldox's mother was concerned. He was always running off to sea on one wild scheme or another.'

'You mean he was a pirate, too?' asked Dana.

Liski Lup nodded. 'More or less. Eventually, Maldox's mother came to loathe humans so much that she rewrote the song Maldox's father sang him to sleep with so every thing in the cosmos would know exactly how she felt about Earth.'

' "Twinkle, Twinkle, Little Star",' said Dana.

'There you go, Dana Bindle. You can pay attention when you try.' Liski began to tap out the tune on the bars with her tube. *'Implode, implode, dying star,'* she sang, *'now I know just what you are. Up above your planets nine, how I wish that you were mine. I would make you cold as space, all your planets I'd erase . . . Implode, implode, dying star, now I know just what you are.'*

Having done so well with paying attention, Dana risked another guess. 'So that's why Maldox and the pirates hate humans so much, because of his mother?'

'I suppose two out of three's not that bad,' said Liski, somehow making it sound as though it were rather worse than bad. 'No, Maldox hates humans because of his father. Because the experiment backfired.' She stopped tapping. 'Maldox blames his father for that.'

Dana was lost again. 'What experiment?'

Liski stopped tapping. 'The experiment in intergalactic breeding, of course.' She leaned forward, resting her hands on her knees. 'You see, it was obvious from the start that humans were going to be trouble,' she explained. 'Culvert Cuvier, you'll remember, knew that eons before there were any humans. By the time there were humans, and they were starting to run all over the Earth blowing each other up and chopping everything else down, the rest of the universe began to get seriously worried. They knew that, in time, it was inevitable that humans would manage to leave their own planet and start mucking around with everyone else's. The sensible Wadrickians thought that if they could add their own genes to the human gene pool, some of the more aggressive and less intelligent human traits might be controlled.'

'It didn't work?' ventured Dana.

'Complete flop.' Liski shook her head sadly. 'Human genes are very dominant. Maldox was the first attempt, but despite his sensible Wadrickian ancestry, I'm afraid that he was always more his father's child.'

Dana was lost again. 'Then why does he hate humans? It doesn't make any sense.'

'It makes perfect sense if you're paying attention,' snapped Liski. 'Once the experiment failed so miserably, Maldox's mother brought him back to Wadric-5. She made him promise that he would never go back to Earth.'

'And he kept his promise?'

'Of course he kept his promise,' said Liski. 'He may be a pirate but he loves his mother. He didn't want to break her heart any more than you would want to break your mother's heart.'

Dana shifted uneasily. Her own mother's heart wouldn't be in very good shape if she could see her daughter now, steaming through space in a pirate ship with a cargo-hold full of lizards and an Intergalactic Trouble Shooter, Grade Z.

'The problem is that Maldox feels much more at home on Earth than he's ever felt on Wadric-5,' Liski continued. 'He claims that it's given him some of his best ideas.' She shrugged. 'I suppose its his *Homo sapiens* genes again, but he seems to admire human spirit and ingenuity. He's crazy about Disneyland.

There's nothing he wants more than to live in California.' She shrugged again. 'Of course, he can't. And that he blames on his father.'

'But that still doesn't make sense,' said Dana slowly. 'If Maldox loves the Earth, and he'd rather be there than on Wadric-5, why isn't it his mother he blames?'

The plum-coloured Lup eyebrows rose. 'Because he's so human, of course. Human logic is a lot like Bombay duck.'

'Bombay duck?'

Liski nodded. 'Bombay duck is fish.' She held her hands out in an empty gesture. 'See what I mean? Human logic. Maldox believes that if his father had been a little more flexible and not fallen out with Maldox's mother, Maldox would have lived on Earth and been able to reach what he feels is his full potential.'

For the first time since she and her cello were thrown in the cell, Dana felt a slight surge of hope. If Maldox the Merciless got his best ideas from humans, then perhaps things weren't as black as they appeared. Perhaps if she had a chance to talk to him and he realized that she was just a little human girl with an aunt who lived in Devon he wouldn't want to make her walk the plank into a black hole after all. Perhaps one of the ideas he'd got was changing your mind.

Dana crossed her fingers. 'So what are Maldox's best ideas?' she asked.

Liski slipped the black tube into the lock of Dana's cell. 'Well, walking the plank for one. Turning urds into handbags, for another. That sort of thing.'

That sort of thing? Hope stopped surging even slightly. Dana uncrossed her fingers.

Liski twiddled the tube back and forth very gently. It startled to gurgle.

'What are you doing?' asked Dana.

'What does it look like I'm doing, baking a cake?' The gurgling grew louder.

'Are you getting me out of here?' Hope returned, and with it excitement. Dana had never been involved in a jail break before. 'Is that what you're doing? Are you getting me out?'

Liski leaned her ear against the tube. 'Do be quiet, Dana Bindle,' she ordered. 'How can I hear with you whining in my ear?'

Dana opened her mouth to say that she wasn't whining, she was just – as usual – trying to discover what was happening, when all at once the ship began to shake in a rather disturbing way.

'What's that?' whispered Dana.

'Sounds like we're stopping. We must be near a black hole.' Still leaning against the tube, Liski consulted her palm. 'Yes,' she said, 'we're within range.'

Dana peered through the bars. She could just make out a large silver disc surrounded by stars shining against the darkness of Liski Lup's skin. The flag of Maldox the Merciless and his pirates was painted on the side of the disc. Instead of a skull and crossbones it was an urd handbag, stuffed with money.

It was amazing how quickly everything moved in space. Already, Dana's excitement about being involved in a jail break had changed to something else: terror.

'Now what?' she asked.

Liski continued to watch as the picture on her palm changed. 'Now Maldox and his thugs make you walk the plank, I should think.' She closed her hand and turned to Dana. 'This sort of situation is the other thing a Beda-X Dematerializer is good for.' She glared crossly at the cello. 'With a Beda-X Dematerializer, we could just vanish from here.'

Dana scowled. Why was everything always *her* fault? 'Don't look at me—'

'There's no time for your excuses now,' snapped Liski. 'They're on their way. Remember that old Zengian saying: *When you can't disappear, then rush to the rear.*'

There was the softest of clicking sounds and the door to Dana's cell swung open. At almost the same nanosecond, quite a few pirates, some of them still wearing their party hats, materialized at the end of the corridor. They were waving maser-lasers and making quite a bit of noise.

Liski Lup gathered up her bags. *'Don't act like a tree. Quick, follow me!'* she cried. And with that she started running in the opposite direction from Maldox's men.

Dana grabbed her cello and sprinted after her. She followed Liski down the twisting corridor, which led to several other twisting corridors, until at last they reached a glowing railing. Liski jumped over the railing like a horse clearing a hedge. Dana put her cello over and jumped too. By the time she picked herself up, Liski Lup was drawing a circle on the wall in front of them with a bright purple crayon.

'What are you doing drawing a picture at a time like this?' whispered Dana.

'Do try to pay attention, Dana Bindle.' Liski began to fill in the circle. 'This isn't a picture, it's a hole.'

Picture, hole, what was the difference? Why would anyone want to stand around drawing anything when there were so many very annoyed pirates chasing her? The racket behind them was getting louder.

'A hole?'

'What else?' sked Liski. *'It's what we need if the urds are to be freed.'* She dropped the crayon into one of her bags and climbed through the hole she'd drawn on the wall. She beckoned. 'Come on!' she said. 'Climb in.'

Dana hesitated. Every time she did what Liski Lup told her to do, she got into trouble.

'What are you waiting for?' hissed Liski Lup. 'The next millennium?'

Besides the fact that Dana was tired of getting into trouble, it didn't seem to her that Liski's hole really looked like a hole, it looked like a purple circle drawn on the wall.

'There it is!' bellowed an angry voice, not nearly far away enough.

Dana looked up. Maldox the Merciless was standing on a walkway high above them, pointing his silver peashooter at her. He didn't look nearly as happy as he had at the party.

'Get it!' roared Maldox. He raised the peashooter. 'It's time the human walked the plank!' He took aim.

Dana could tell that, this time, he wouldn't miss. Dana stopped hesitating and scrambled into the wall.

She and her cello landed in a dark, narrow tunnel. It was difficult to see because the only light was the colour of currants. It was impossible to stand up because the tunnel was so low. She could just make out the Intergalactic Trouble Shooter, Grade Z, sitting a few feet away from her on a raft of carrier bags. She was wearing a shining blue helmet, dusted with silver glitter.

'Pull it after you!' shouted Liski Lup.

Now what's she on about? wondered Dana. 'Pull what after me?' she shouted back.

'The hole, of course! Quickly! Pull it in!'

The high-pitched, red beams of the maser-lasers started flashing across the opening. One of them missed Dana's ear by only millimetres. She didn't need to be told three times. Dana pulled. Much to her surprise, she found herself staring back at a blank wall and clutching a small purple hole.

'Now get on!'

Holding the hole with one hand and the cello with the other, Dana hastily climbed on behind Liski Lup. The bags sagged. There was something in the way they sagged that made Dana think there was nothing beneath them.

Floating on nothing on a raft of carrier bags didn't really appeal to her that much. 'I don't think—' began Dana.

Liski handed her a helmet. *'Don't stop to think! Jump into the drink!'* she yelled.

'What drink?' asked Dana, wondering if it was too late to change her mind and get off.

It was.

The pirates started pounding angrily on the wall as the carrier-bag raft containing Liski Lup, Dana Bindle and Dana Bindle's cello, shot forwards – or perhaps it was backwards.

CHAPTER NINE

Going with the Flow

The makeshift raft was twisting, looping, and spinning through the tunnel like a leaf caught in the wind. Liski Lup was talking. Dana wasn't listening. Dana was wondering if she was going to be sick. Last summer her father had taken her on the giant rollercoaster at the shore and she'd been sick. She'd thrown up all over his new shoes. Next to this ride, however, the giant rollercoaster had been like sitting on a blanket in the back garden. Then, too, there hadn't been any pirates chasing them. Dana might not know where they were, but the pirates did and had finally managed to find a way into the tunnel.

To stop herself from thinking about being sick, Dana decided to pay attention. It might be a good idea to discover exactly where they were, what was happening, and where they were going.

'What did you say we're in?' asked Dana.

'Mmphgnnpfrrrt,' said Liski Lup.

Perhaps it was because of the helmet, or the whooshing echo, or the wailing of the maser-lasers; or perhaps it was because she wasn't finding it easy to keep herself and her cello on the carrier bags, but even when she was paying attention Dana was having trouble hearing.

Another burst of ruby beams from the pirates weapons flashed behind them. Dana resisted the urge to turn around. She was terrified enough without discovering just how near Maldox and his men really were.

'A what?' screamed Dana.

'Mmphgnnpfrrrt,' said Liski Lup.

'*What?*'

The raft suddenly turned on its side, a trick it hadn't performed before, and began to ride the tunnel wall. For the first time in her life, Dana was glad she hadn't had much to eat.

'Macromagnetic reactor!' Liski shouted. 'We're in the ship's power centre. I knew Maldox would have his own way in, of course, but we did have a head start, and it's difficult for them to catch up with us here.'

Which answered one of Dana's questions.

'That's why we have so much velocity and no control,' Liski explained. 'We're free-wheeling.'

Which answered another.

Hugging her cello as though it were an anchor and not just something else that was free-wheeling on the raft, Dana asked her third question. 'But where does it *go*?'

More shots pulsated crazily around them.

'Like most things in the universe, it doesn't *go* anywhere,' yelled Liski Lup. 'It just *is*.'

That wasn't really what Dana wanted to hear. She'd been hoping that the tunnel lead somewhere – somewhere quiet, static and pirate-free.

'Are you saying that we're going absolutely nowhere as fast as possible?'

The raft took another turn, this time skimming along the ceiling. It occurred to Dana as she clutched her cello that it was a shame she'd never wanted to know what it was like to travel perpendicularly at a very great speed since she now had the rare opportunity of finding out. Dana had never given it much thought before, but she suddenly understood exactly what the phrase 'my heart was in my mouth' meant. Given the fact that they were hanging upside down there was no other place where her heart might be.

'Something like that,' said Liski casually, as though it really didn't matter.

It mattered to Dana. 'But what about the pirates?' she screeched as another round of maser-laser fire shrieked and glowed around them. 'They're catching up!'

Liski refused to share Dana's increasing sense of panic and doom. 'No, they aren't,' she said flatly. 'They're free-wheeling, too. At this specific point in time, they don't really know where they are, never mind where we are.'

Does that make me feel better or not? Dana wondered as the raft started revolving around the sides of the tunnel.

'You know, this reminds me a lot of star surfing,' said Liski as they spun. From the tone of her voice, you'd think that they were sitting on a double-decker bus having a friendly chat.

'It reminds me of falling through a black hole,' gasped Dana.

Liski shook her head. 'Nothing like it.' She glanced over her shoulder. 'I used to star surf a lot when I was your age, you know. It's excellent for concentrating the mind. Perhaps you should try it sometime.'

Dana was about to ask how anything this terrifying

could be excellent for concentrating anything, when the tunnel suddenly dropped away.

'Oops,' said Liski Lup.

Dana screamed.

The raft containing Liski Lup, Dana Bindle, and Dana Bindle's cello fell straight down, rather like a rock thrown from a tower. Unlike a rock thrown from a tower, they seemed to be hurtling through very cold jelly. And not lime jelly, either, which was Dana's favourite, but strawberry, which wasn't.

'What is this stuff?' gasped Dana in a small, choked voice.

Still behaving as though she were on a double-decker stuck in traffic on the high street, Liski Lup was busily sorting through one of her bags.

'Talk about the luck of a lepton!' she said with a laugh, sounding very pleased. 'You see what happens when you go with the flow? Chance is so productive. I couldn't have planned it better myself.' She removed a handful of bright orange balls. 'It's as the Thrums always say: *If it's going to happen, it will.*'

'I don't care what the Thrums always say,' panted Dana. 'I want to know what *is* happening. Where are we going now?'

Liski laughed. '*Well, we're not going up, or I'm no Lup!*' she chortled.

The jelly seemed to be getting warmer.

'But where *are* we going?' Dana repeated.

The jelly started to melt. Dana started to sweat. The raft started picking up speed.

'Now what?' screamed Dana.

'Perfect! Perfect! Perfect,' giggled Liski Lup. 'Here, take these interference orbs.' She held up two of the orange balls.

Dana looked at them. Had Liski gone completely mad? There was no way Dana was going to let go of either the raft or her cello to hold some rubber balls. 'I can't!' she yelled. 'I only have two hands, you know.'

'Humans,' said Liski Lup, as though this, too, were Dana's fault. 'Suit yourself.'

Down, down, down they went . . . faster and faster . . . down and down. It was getting hotter and hotter and more and more humid. Dana wondered if they were coming to a beach, though that did seem unlikely, even here.

Liski Lup raised her arms over her head, an orange ball in each hand. The balls were luminescing and growing in size.

It seemed to Dana that she'd missed something important about these balls. 'What are those things?' she asked.

'I told you,' said Liski. 'Interference orbs.'

'Yes, I know *that*,' said Dana. 'I meant what do they do?'

'Do?' snapped Liski. 'Do? Why, they break your fall, of course. I, myself, would never travel any- where without them.' She sniffed. 'Nor would anyone with any sense,' she added pointedly.

It was at exactly that point in time that everything went black. When Dana came round she was lying on something that might be very deep grass. Or, given the weirdness of outer space, might not be very deep grass. Odd sounds – part whirrs and part squeaks – were coming from every direction.

Dana's eyes opened slowly. Her bottom hurt, she had a bump on her head, she was sweating, and she couldn't see anything. Dana blinked several times. She still couldn't see anything.

'Liski?' called Dana, immediately panicking. 'Liski, I'm blind!'

'There you go, leaping to the wrong conclusions again,' a familiar voice shouted over the whirrs and squeaks. 'Don't you ever learn anything?'

What do I have to do to get some sympathy from her? wondered Dana. *She probably won't even feel sorry when they make me walk the plank.*

'What do you mean "the wrong conclusion"?' Dana yelled back. 'I can't see! What other conclusion is there but that I'm blind?'

'To every question there are hundreds of answers,' said Liski. A hand grabbed Dana's arm and pulled her to her feet. 'Of course you can't see,' she snapped, as though this, too, were something Dana shouldn't need to be told. 'This is a simulated night swamp. You're not supposed to be able to see unless you're an urd.'

'A simulated what?'

Not only was the noise annoying, but there was the most peculiar smell. It reminded Dana of something that had been sitting on the bottom of a lake for a very long time.

'Night swamp. Here, take this while I get out a light.' She thrust what seemed to be a large jar into Dana's hands.

'What is it?' asked Dana.

'Baloofas.'

Dana had a vague memory of the word 'baloofa' being mentioned before, but she couldn't quite remember in what context. Maybe it was some sort of weapon.

'Baloofas?' Dana repeated.

There was a sizzle and a pop, and then a bright purple light illuminated the room. The squeaks and whirrs grew louder and more hysterical. Dana blinked. Liski Lup, holding a glowing U-shaped bulb over her head, was smiling at her.

'There,' said Liski. 'That's better.'

'Better?' asked Dana. She stared down at the thing in her hand. It wasn't a weapon. It was a jar filled with thousands – maybe even millions – of very small and very black creatures. The creatures had a great number of waving antennae and legs. 'This is better?' *Better than what?* It was as much as Dana could manage not to drop the jar and start screaming.

'Baloofa bugs,' said Liski. 'You know . . . For the urds.'

The urds? Very, very slowly, and very, very carefully, Dana moved her eyes from the baloofa bugs. The room they were in – which, indeed, was a swamp – was packed with urds. There were thousands of them, too. Because of the suction cups on the bottoms of their feet, they not only scampered across the marshy ground, but they hung from vines, they clung to rocks, they dangled from trees, and they raced across the ceiling and walls.

Something brushed against her leg. Dana looked down. More urds. There were even several dozen on her cello. They were all squeaking and whirring, and staring at her with their protruding black eyes. They might be an endangered species, but they certainly weren't what you could call attractive. They certainly weren't what Dana would call attractive.

'What's wrong with them?' Dana wished there was somewhere she could go that would be out of the way of the urds, but every time she moved a centimetre the urds moved a centimetre, too.

'What's wrong with them?' asked Liski crossly. 'What do you think's wrong with them? They're hungry, and they're frightened, and their prison hasn't been cleaned for weeks by the smell of it.' She started rummaging through her bags again. 'Those pirates never feed them. They don't care if they starve or not. Maldox never was known for his sensitivity to others,' she grumbled. She produced another jar of baloofa bugs with a triumphant flourish. 'And, of course, they're overcrowded. Urds aren't urban humans, you know. They don't like to be all on top of one another like this. It upsets them.'

It was upsetting Dana too.

'Hungry?' said Dana. She looked at the jar in her hand. That familiar golf-club feeling came over her again. The urds moved towards her. 'What do you want me to do?'

'Why, feed them, of course.' She shoved the second jar into Dana's hand. 'I have to find a way out of here before the pirates realize where we are.'

'Feed them?'

'What are you, my echo?' snapped Liski. 'Yes, feed them. You can see that the poor little things haven't had a decent meal in days.'

Dana stared at her companion in horror. 'But I can't feed them baloofa bugs,' she protested. 'I'm practically a vegetarian. *And* I'm against fox hunting.'

'Well, then, there's no problem, is there?' smiled Liski. 'They aren't foxes, they're baloofa bugs, and no one expects or wants *you* to eat them.'

'But they're alive!'

Liski thrust another jar at her. 'Of course they're alive. Urds can't eat them if they're dead, they can't digest them properly.'

'But—'

'But, but, but,' cut in Liski Lup. 'You're the buttiest little girl I've ever met.' She put her hands on her hips and looked at Dana. Her eyes flashed. 'Humans hunt foxes because they think it's fun to scare some defenceless creature out of its brain and exercise their horses at the same time. Urds eat baloofa bugs in order to live and to control the baloofa bug population so it doesn't self-destruct. There's a very big difference between those two things, Dana Bindle,' said Liski sternly. 'And the quicker you understand that difference, the better off we'll all be.'

Dana opened her mouth to argue some more; all she could think to say was 'but', so she closed it again.

Liski handed her a carrier bag. 'You'll find all the baloofa bugs you need in here,' she said. She started to walk away. 'Now, if I were you, I'd feed the urds immediately. I don't imagine we have too much time. Eventually Maldox will figure out that we must have fallen into an emergency escape hatch, and he'll know exactly where we are.' She pushed back a giant plant and turned to Dana. 'Remember,' she said.

91

'Maldox is not only merciless, he's rather intelligent for a half-human.' And then, just before she vanished, added, 'Of course, he does come from good genetic make-up on his mother's side.'

CHAPTER TEN

Everything Falls into Place Except Dana, Who Falls Out

Liski Lup reappeared just as Dana was wondering if the urd diet really was restricted exclusively to baloofa bugs, or if it stretched to include human children during emergencies. Liski Lup had a pink and purple orchid pinned to her collar. 'You see how everything falls into place if you give it a chance?' she was saying.

As relieved as Dana was to see the Intergalactic Trouble Shooter again, she wasn't really listening to what the Intergalactic Trouble Shooter was saying. Instead, Dana was standing behind her cello, trying her best to get away from the urds. Although they'd gobbled up the baloofa bugs in about half a nano-second, they still seemed to be hungry. Liski Lup, however, had been right: Dana's best wasn't all that good. She couldn't get away from the urds. They had her surrounded. There were even several standing up against Dana's cello, squeaking and whirring in Dana's direction. Either they were still hungry, or they liked her, which wasn't a comforting thought either.

Liski rattled on. 'Although you disobeyed me and brought attention to yourself, we still got where we wanted to be,' she was explaining. 'Although I had to give myself away because you were in jail, we still found the urds.' She clapped her hands together.

'Now all we have to do is get the urds out of here, take over the ship, drop Maldox and his men into that black hole they've so conveniently stopped by, and we'll be on our way.'

Something Liski had just said finally caught Dana's attention. She stopped worrying about the urds and stared at Liski. 'What do you mean *take over the ship*?'

'I do wish you'd listen, Dana,' snapped Liski Lup impatiently. 'Of course we have to take over the ship. What did you think we were going to do? Wait for Maldox to *give* it to us?'

Dana scowled. Perhaps it was true that she didn't always pay as much attention as she should, but no one could expect her to pay attention when multi-coloured lizards with horns were trying to climb all over her.

'But why do we have to take over the ship?' she asked. 'Why can't we just hide till we land?'

'If we wait till we land, you and I will have less chance of escaping than a baloofa bug would have of surviving an urd banquet,' said Liski. 'They'll surround the ship and then they'll turn off the heat and freeze us out.' She straightened her orchid. 'No, we'll have to fight them for the ship.'

'But, do we have to fight the pirates?' asked Dana. Fleeing the pirates was hard enough. She didn't really fancy fighting them. 'Can't we just wait till they're asleep or something?'

'*Evil never sleeps, it creeps*,' chanted Liski. 'And besides, you don't think Maldox is going to take a nap now, when he knows there's a human and a Grade Z Intergalactic Trouble Shooter on board, do you?'

'I suppose not,' answered Dana. She could see that their presence on the ship might keep Maldox awake. It was like the time she thought there was a ghost in her room. It had taken her hours to get to sleep.

'I'm glad you're finally thinking clearly,' said Liski. 'There's no other way.'

Dana wasn't convinced. There had to be another way. One of the urds was climbing up Dana's cello, but Dana was so busy thinking of reasons for not taking over the ship that she didn't flinch. A reason came to her. 'But, surely, if they don't know where we are—'

Liski Lup interrupted. 'Oh, they know by now,' she said matter-of-factly. 'The pirates of Wadric-5 aren't like you, Dana Bindle. They pay attention. So part of the bad news is that we're not really hiding.'

'We're not?'

Liski's stars shook. 'No, we're not.'

'What are we then?' asked Dana in a very soft voice. It was a question she didn't really want to ask, but she felt someone had to.

'We're trapped.'

Dana couldn't wait to hear what the other part of the bad news was. She didn't have long to wait.

'And the other part of the bad news,' Liski continued, 'is that at this specific point in time there isn't any way out of here. All the escape routes are blocked with the anti-lac gel we came through so the urds can't get away.'

Dana perked up. That didn't seem like such bad news to her. 'Then why don't we just leave them there?' she asked. 'We can always come back for them later.'

'There won't *be* any later if we don't have the urds with us,' Liski Lup informed her. 'The urds are the only thing we have in our favour. Maldox is afraid of urds.'

'Really?' Dana was surprised. She didn't really care for urds herself, but she would have thought that someone whose last name was Merciless must be tougher than that.

'Can't stand them,' said Liski. 'None of the pirates can, of course, but with Maldox it's a phobia. If he were all human I suppose it would be spiders he'd be terrified of, but as he isn't all human it's urds.' She picked up several urds in one hand and kissed them on their bumpy little heads. 'I don't understand it myself, of course. When I look at an urd I see intelligence, harmony and beauty. But when Maldox looks at one, the first thing he sees is an ugly lizard and the second is a handbag.'

The urd that had been climbing Dana's cello reached the top and sat there looking at her quizzically. Its skin glowed and its urd eyes swivelled. Dana could understand how anyone might look at an urd and see a rather ugly lizard; what she couldn't understand was how you could look at one and see a handbag. None of her mother's handbags were green with blobs of purple, blue and yellow and the texture of gravel.

'And what happens if we just stay where we are?' asked Dana, still thinking. 'Surely the pirates aren't going to come down after us if they're that afraid of urds.'

'What happens if we stay here?' Liski shrugged. 'Who can say what will happen? One thing or another. But probably you're right for a change. Probably the pirates won't come down. It's much more likely that they'll just open the floor, turn on the number ten anti-personnel vacuum, and wait for us to drip into their laps.'

Now that did seem like a bit of a problem.

Do I really want to know what a number ten anti-personnel vacuum is? Dana asked herself. She decided that she didn't; what she imagined was awful enough. She decided to ask a different question.

'But what about the urds? The pirates aren't going to want the urds to drop into their laps.'

'The urds won't drop into their laps.' Liski's voice was slightly muffled, as her head was in a bag. 'The urds will automatically suction themselves onto something solid as soon as the number ten anti-personnel vacuum is turned on.'

'Oh,' said Dana. There really didn't seem much else she could say.

'Now, where is that solar adjustor?' Liski muttered to herself, almost disappearing inside the bag. 'It's always the same when you pack in a hurry. You never remember where anything is.' She raised her head to look at Dana. 'Meanwhile, get out your cello and get ready to play,' she ordered.

The urd on Dana's shoulder was leaning its head against hers. All of a sudden it reminded Dana a little of her dog back home. Not that her dog sounded like a faulty smoke alarm.

'Play?' repeated Dana. 'Play what?'

'I thought there was only one thing you could

play,' said Liski. 'Which of course, as chance would have it, is perfect for our purpose.'

'"Twinkle, Twinkle, Little Star"?'

'Exactly. The urds are very musical, you know. If anything can drive them out of here, that's the tune. It'll take too long if we wait for them to leave by themselves.'

'But I thought you said there was no way out. You said all the exits are sealed with anti-lac gel.'

Liski Lup sighed dramatically. 'Do try to pay attention for a change, Dana Bindle. It's not just your life that's at stake here. The fate of an entire planet rests on us.'

'I was paying attention,' protested Dana. 'All I said was—'

Dana's sentence was drowned out by Liski Lup's cry of delight. 'Here we are!' She held up a small pink and yellow box.

Dana stared at the box. It looked as though it might contain chocolates. 'What is it?' she asked. The urd on her shoulder was falling asleep.

Liski made a disgusted face. 'How many times do I have to tell you to listen? Didn't I just say it was a solar adjustor?' She held up the box and it began to shine. 'With this I can melt the anti-lac gel and make the escape route acceptable for urds.' She raised her eyebrows. 'All you have to do is make them want to leave.'

Dana knew she wasn't a very good cellist – how could she not know that when Mrs Preski was always telling her she wasn't – but she still felt a little hurt that Liski Lup thought the only use her playing had was for scaring off urds. Her mother wouldn't be too happy about it either. Her mother had hoped she'd play in an orchestra, not become lizard repellent.

Liski smiled at her. 'You see?' she said happily. 'Everything has a purpose in the cosmos, even you and your cello.' She waved one hand over Dana's head. 'But before you begin, I'd get up a bit higher, if I were you. Go to the top of one of those trees.'

Dana looked up. The trees under discussion seemed terribly high. 'Climb, you mean?' she squeaked.

Liski dived into another carrier bag. 'Unless you can fly, it would seem like the easiest way.' She pulled out what looked like a pair of chopsticks and leaned them against the tallest tree. Green lights rose from the chopsticks, twisting their way up the trunk of the tree. 'Use that,' said Liski. 'It's a ladder laser.'

'But, Liski Lup,' began Dana, 'I can't climb two thin green lights. It's not possible. I weigh nearly five stone.' Was there nothing Liski Lup considered too ridiculous for Dana to undertake?

Apparently not.

'Now,' said Liski, 'as even you should know, Dana Bindle, when the gel melts it'll turn to liquid. Quite a lot of liquid, actually.' She pulled out a pair of gold and silver wellies. 'Considering how hard it is for you to play the cello under normal circumstances, I shouldn't think that being several metres under liquid anti-lac would help much.'

Dana didn't think it would help much, either. She looked at the laser ladder. It was now the green of vines and thicker than her wrist. She looked at the urd on her shoulder. It was snoring. She looked at Liski Lup. Liski Lup was putting on the boots.

'My advice would be to take it out of its case now,' said Liski.

Dana took the cello out of its case. She put the bow between her teeth. She heaved the cello into her arms.

If I ever get back home, I'll never ever complain about having to take my cello to school again, Dana promised herself as she started up the laser ladder. Even squeezing onto a crowded bus with a cello was a lot easier than hauling one up a very large tree on a laser ladder. *I mean it*, thought Dana as the ladder wheezed and swayed. *I'll never complain about my lessons, either, or about Mrs Preski* . . . The higher she climbed, the darker it got, and the thicker and more humid the air became. Thousands of insects no larger than specks of dust were trying to fly up her nose and into her eyes. She started to sneeze. *And I'll practise*, she further promised. *I'll practise every day.*

Out of breath and still sneezing, Dana stopped at a crook in the tree. She looked down. Liski Lup was gathering her bags together. 'Is this high enough?' called Dana.

'Higher!' was the immediate reply.

'She could at least have looked to see how high up I am,' grumbled Dana as she started climbing again.

At the next branch that seemed large enough to hold her and her cello, Dana stopped again. She looked down. She could see plenty of urds, but no sign of the Intergalactic Trouble Shooter, Grade Z.

'Here?' shouted Dana.

The voice of Liski Lup boomed at her from across the swamp. 'Start playing!' it ordered. 'Start playing now!'

'Start playing now!' grumbled Dana. She heaved herself and her cello onto the branch. 'That's all very well for you to say.' It had never occurred to her how difficult it would be to balance a cello at the top of a jungle tree. Playing up here wasn't going to help her performance, that much was certain.

'When I say now I don't mean later!' roared Liski.

Leaning gingerly against several branches behind her, Dana took up her bow. She held it the way Mrs Preski had shown her. She bent her elbow. She put her fingers in position on the frets. Something rustled. The lizard suddenly jumped off her shoulder onto a branch. Dana and her cello started to fall.

It was much easier going back down than it had been going up.

Just as long as I don't land on dozens of urds, thought Dana as she and her cello rushed towards the floor. *Just as long as I land on something soft but inanimate.*

She landed on nothing. Instead of stopping when she reached the ground, Dana kept right on going. She was back in the strawberry jelly. She must have found an escape route that Liski had missed.

'Now where am I going,' wailed Dana as she continued to fall.

As was usual in deepest space, she didn't have long to wait for an answer.

There was a sudden explosion of light and sound as Dana and her cello burst through a wall of darkness and finally came to a stop on something solid.

'Well, look who's here,' said a warm, unfriendly voice.

Dana opened her eyes.

Maldox the Merciless was sitting in a large black

101

chair only centimetres from where she'd landed. He was smiling and slapping a long, thick stick against the palm of his hand. His men stood beside him, smiling, too.

Dana's eyes went back to the stick. It was brown and black and had a silver paddle at one end. Dana blinked. The initials A. B. were written in gold on the handle. The last time she'd seen that black and brown stick, that silver paddle and those gold initials they'd been heading towards the bottom of a lake. She blinked again. It couldn't be, but it did seem to be . . .

'Never mind me,' said Dana, too surprised to be frightened. 'What are you doing with my father's golf club?'

CHAPTER ELEVEN

There's Nothing Like a Game of Golf

As soon as the words 'What are you doing with my father's golf club?' were out of her mouth, Dana wondered if she hadn't made another mistake. The question didn't improve the pirate's mood.

'What?' said Maldox.

Somehow, it didn't sound to Dana as if he were asking her something, it sounded as if he was making a threat.

'That's my father's golf club,' she repeated, a little more politely. 'It has his initials on it. A. B. – for Arthur Bindle.'

Maldox leaned forward, his chocolate-digestive eyes gleaming with a new interest. 'Golf?' he said, completely ignoring the matter of whose club it was. 'Do you play golf?'

Dana didn't play golf. Her father had tried to teach her several times, but her father lacked the patience and persistence of Mrs Iris Preski, who would never give up and admit that Dana's talent for the cello was less than a chicken's for sky diving, and that she was much more suited for the guitar. Her father had given up, admitting that Dana was more suited for landscape gardening. 'The way you swing,' said her father, 'you should be trimming the edge of the lawn.'

Dana could tell that now was a very good point in time to pay attention. She thought about Maldox's question, trying to determine what the right answer might be. If she said she didn't play golf she would probably be thrown into space without any further delay. If she said that she played golf . . . Dana concentrated. Perhaps, like Dana's father, once you started Maldox talking about golf he would bang on for hours. If Maldox banged on about golf for hours, Liski Lup would have time to escape and rescue Dana from spending the rest of her life as part of a black hole.

'Well, actually,' said Dana, deciding to tug the truth into a more acceptable shape, 'I have played a little . . .'

Maldox leapt to his feet, more excited now than he'd been at his party. 'Then we'll play a game!' he cried. 'You and I will play a game of golf!'

'We will?' Dana hadn't expected this. A simulated night swamp on a pirate spaceship was one thing, but a golf course seemed extremely peculiar. 'Play golf?'

Maldox waved the club towards his men. 'It's my favourite game,' he said, 'but none of this lot can play worth a neutrino. They keep sending the balls into orbit.'

That's no worse than sending the balls into the lake, thought Dana. She had the unhappy suspicion that playing with Maldox wasn't going to be any more fun than playing with Arthur Bindle.

Maldox lifted her and her cello from the floor. 'Then that's decided!' he said cheerfully. 'You and I will play a game before you walk the plank!'

When are things going to fall into place? wondered Dana.

Not soon, apparently.

Maldox was laughing. 'Happy birthday to me!' he said gleefully. 'I had a great party, I captured a human, I finally have that interfering Liski Lup where I want her, and now I'm going to play golf! What a day!'

You think you've had a day, thought Dana. *What about me?* She put a disappointed expression on her face. 'I'd love to play with you, I really would,' she said, sounding regretful. 'But I'm afraid that I forgot to bring a club with me.'

Maldox gestured to his pirates again. 'They've sent all the clubs into orbit too,' he said sourly, 'or I'd offer you one of ours.' His eyes fell on the cello. He grinned. 'You can use that!'

Before Dana could even consider whether or not she should try to stop him, Maldox grabbed the cello out of her arms.

'But that—' bleated Dana.

Before you could say 'gluon', he'd snapped off the neck.

'It's perfect,' said Maldox. He held up the broken length of cello proudly. 'It's the right size and everything.' He thrust it into Dana's hand. 'I'll meet you on the course in ten minutes,' he said. 'I have to get my cap.'

Dana stared glumly at the strings dangling sadly from the cello's neck. For the first time, walking the plank didn't seem like such a horrible idea. If Dana returned home with a broken cello her mother would probably murder her anyway.

*

Why isn't Liski Lup ever around when I really need her?
This thought occurred to Dana several hours into her
game with Maldox the Merciless, while she was
staring hopelessly at the pompom on top of Maldox's
cap. Maldox's cap was red, green and yellow tartan,
and clearly made for someone with less hair and
shorter ears. It didn't suit him.

Dana sighed silently as Maldox whacked a ball
towards the flag numbered one. Golf didn't suit
Maldox, either. The ball sailed past the flag, vanished
into the far end of the ship, and then came rico-
cheting back. Everyone would have ducked if they
hadn't been ducking already, but there were several
other balls travelling up and down the course in the
same way, and all of the spectators had hit the
ground the second the first one took to the air. The
only one who wasn't ducking was a deep-plum-
coloured pirate with a green eye-patch who was
sitting on a high platform at one end of the room,
acting as umpire.

*It was a mistake. I should never have mentioned the golf
club*, thought Dana, covering her head as the ball
whizzed past over it. *I should have let them hurl me into
a black hole. It couldn't possibly be worse than this*.

Dana's father always claimed that golf was the
perfect sport because it was calm, gentlemanly,
ordered, unstressful and non-aggressive, and
depended not on chance but on skill and control.
There was nothing like a game of golf for relaxing,
said Arthur Bindle.

Of course, Dana's father had never played with
Maldox the Merciless on a metal links in the belly of

an alien spacecraft. If he had, he might have changed his mind.

There was nothing relaxing about the way Maldox played. Maldox was not calm. He was not gentlemanly. He was not ordered. And he certainly was stressed and aggressive. He also played a different version of golf than that played at the Rolling Green Golf Club, where Arthur Bindle played. For one thing, although they'd been playing for hours, Dana hadn't yet had a turn. For another thing, Maldox made up the rules as he went along. For yet another thing, he didn't believe that the game depended on skill and control, but on getting as many balls flying back and forth in the air as possible, until one of them finally lost its momentum and fell into a hole. There was something about Maldox that reminded her of someone else, but she couldn't quite work out who it was.

As the last ball thudded to the floor of the ship, the pirates got to their feet, cheering. Dana wasn't sure if they were cheering because they actually believed that Maldox had done well, or if they were cheering because they didn't have to play with him. She suspected the latter was closest to the truth.

'Well done, Maldox,' said Cayman the Cruel, who was acting as ball carrier. 'You nearly got one in that time.'

'It was close, wasn't it?' asked Maldox. 'I do think the probability ratio's going up.' He adjusted his hat. 'My game must be improving.'

Dana doubted that. It seemed much more likely that the balls were getting tired, too.

Maldox stepped back from the tee. 'Your turn, Dana Bindle!' he shouted. 'Let's see how well you do.'

Dana had been dreading this moment. She'd already been warned that the last thing she wanted to do was well. Cayman the Cruel had warned her. He'd taken her aside while Maldox was getting his cap. 'Whatever you do, don't put a ball down a hole,' he'd told her. Dana's grasp on the finer points of golf was a little shaky, but she was pretty certain that getting the ball down the hole was actually the object of the game. 'Because it'll make Maldox mad,' Cayman had informed her when she'd asked why not. 'He hates to lose.' Dana had pointed out that it really didn't matter to her whether or not Maldox got mad, since he was going to dump her in a black hole anyway. Cayman had arched one eyebrow. 'If you make Maldox mad, you'll be lucky to end up in a black hole,' he'd said.

Maldox started pounding Dana's father's club on the ground. 'Shake a few molecules, Dana Bindle!' he ordered. 'We don't have eternity to wait for you, you know.'

But we had eternity to wait for you, thought Dana sourly. She frowned. All at once, she knew whom it was that Maldox reminded her of. As weird as things were once you left the Earth's orbit, how was it possible that Maldox the Merciless could sound so much like Liski Lup?

'Well, I waited quite a long while for you, you know,' she muttered, forgetting for just the jump of an electron that he wasn't Liski.

Maldox raised the club, pointing it at her heart.

'Let's remember who's the pirate chief around here and who's the prisoner,' he said.

As if Dana could forget.

Cautiously, she stepped up to the tee. Cayman handed her a fluorescent yellow ball. She put it in position. She looked at the hole ahead of her. She looked at the end of her cello. *Aim for the wall*, she told herself. *Aim for the wall*. Dana aimed. She swung.

The main reason Dana's father had given up trying to teach her to play golf was because she never hit anything she aimed for. She hit the golf cart. She hit trees. She once even hit her father, but she never got anywhere near the hole.

Except this time. This time, the ball went straight for the flag numbered one, and into the cup.

The effect was instantaneous.

'That's it!' screamed Maldox. 'I've had enough of this! I'm not playing any more!' He raised the club. 'And, as for you, Dana Bindle, just wait till you see what happens to humans who cheat on my ship!'

Dana wondered whether she should try to explain that her hole in one was an accident or whether she should run.

'Walking the plank's too good for you!' roared Maldox. The club soared through the air, heading for Dana.

She ran.

The pirates started running, too.

'Fifty urds to the pirate who catches that human brat!' shrieked Maldox.

Don't look back, Dana told herself as she raced towards the door she'd come in. *Just run, run, run*.

It was at precisely that point in time when Dana

tripped over her father's golf club that she realized the door was gone.

'Oof!' gasped Dana. The cello neck flew out of her hand, she crashed into the wall.

And at precisely that point in time, the wall Dana had hit slid open and Liski Lup, several thousand urds, and a great deal of water, poured into Maldox's golf course.

Maldox started bellowing. 'I'll get you for this, Liski Lup!' he roared. 'Don't you worry, I'll get you for this!'

The Intergalactic Trouble Shooter landed lightly next to Dana. 'What took you so long?' asked Liski Lup.

CHAPTER TWELVE

Things Have a Way of Working Out

On Dana's bureau at home was a glass ball her aunt had brought her from a beach holiday. Inside the glass ball was an underwater scene of sand made out of glitter, plastic seaweed, a plastic sunken ship, and tiny plastic fish and shells in a clear liquid. When you shook the ball, the sand filled it and the fish and shells floated about wildly. Dana had never given much thought before to what it would be like to be inside that ball when someone started shaking it, but she thought about it now. She thought it must be a lot like being trapped in the flooded belly of a Wadrickian pirate ship, surrounded by hysterical urds leaping and diving and shrieking like broken doorbells, and panicky pirates splashing and shouting and firing their space guns in every direction.

Dana pushed a few dozen urds away and groped behind her for something to hold on to. There was nothing there.

'Liski,' whispered Dana. 'Liski, how does Maldox know who you are?'

'It's a small cosmos,' answered Liski. 'And besides, Maldox and I go back a long way. If there's something after him, it's usually me.'

'So now what happens?' asked Dana. 'Do we give ourselves up?'

'Give up?' Liski glared at her over the pink and

orange goggles she was wearing now. 'Intergalactic Trouble Shooters and their apprentices do not give up, Dana Bindle. Surrender is not in our vocabulary.'

'Well, it's in my vocabulary,' she replied a little sharply. The pirates were recovering from their surprise and fright and were beginning to assemble on top of the umpire's platform.

'Then get rid of it,' advised Liski Lup.

'But, Liski,' Dana argued, 'what can we possibly do except surrender? We're outnumbered. We're unarmed. It's their ship . . .'

'It's simple, really,' said Liski Lup. 'All we have to do is get the pirates into the shuttle, put it on a course that will take it straight to the black hole, and we can be on our way.'

'Oh, is that all?' gasped Dana. It didn't seem simple to her. The pirates had all reached the safety of the platform, but the urds were still churning crazily around each other, just like the sand, fish and shells in the glass ball back on Hollyrod Drive.

Liski nodded. 'That's all.' She shoved something metallic into Dana's hand. 'Here,' she said, 'you know what to do.'

'No, I don't,' said Dana. She looked at the thing in her hand. It was a thin piece of wire, two-thirds of which was coated with hardened blue glop. 'What is it?'

'What does it look like?' snapped Liski.

'A sparkler,' said Dana.

Which was true. Although Liski Lup, of course, didn't seem to think so.

Liski snorted. 'It's as the Quechuans always say,'

she said, dodging the ruby beams that had begun to shoot around them, 'you can take a human off the Earth but you can't make her think.'

A wet, whimpering urd landed on Dana's head. As far as thinking went, Dana really didn't think that this was the right time for another lecture.

'Oh, is that what the Quechuans always say?' asked Dana. 'I was wondering what it was.'

Liski Lup, however, didn't think it was the right time for sarcasm.

'*Don't talk, walk,*' she said sharply. She gave Dana a shove. 'Twirl the gravitino gun over your head as fast as you can and it'll create an invisible wall around you. It doesn't have much of a life span, of course, but it should last long enough for you to get Maldox and his mercenaries into the shuttle.'

Besides coming to grips with the gravitino gun, Dana had been trying to dodge the maser-laser rays and watch out for flying urds herself, but something Liski Lup said made her turn her full attention to the Integalactic Trouble Shooter, Grade Z.

'*Me?*' said Dana. 'You're expecting *me* to get the pirates out of the ship?'

Liski picked up her bags. '*There's no one here but me and you, and I must shoo,*' she replied. She started wading towards the hole in the wall that she'd entered by.

'But, where are you going?' demanded Dana.

Liski looked over her shoulder. 'To the control centre, of course. There's no point getting Maldox and his thugs into the shuttle if there's no one to program it into the black hole, is there?'

'Well, no,' said Dana. 'I guess not.' Even someone being hurled about in a glass ball could see the logic of that.

Liski started wading on.

'Hold on!' called Dana. 'What about me? How do I get the pirates off the ship?'

Liski turned impatiently. 'You use the urds, of course. You blew it before, but now I'm giving you a second chance to make yourself useful.' Once more, she began to wade away. 'Play them that silly star song of yours and in their panic to get away from you and your bad music, they'll drive the pirates into the shuttle. There's nowhere else they can go from here. I've sealed all the other exits.'

'But what about the urds?' asked Dana. 'Won't they follow the pirates into the shuttle?'

Liski Lup laughed. 'Why ever would they want to do a silly thing like that for?' she asked.

'But—' began Dana.

'*Shut the buts, it's time to crack nuts*,' chimed Liski.

Under different circumstances, Dana would have found a more indirect, roundabout way to tell Liski about the cello. Unfortunately, the circumstances they were in weren't different, they were rapidly becoming chaotic.

'But the cello's broken,' blurted out Dana.

Liski didn't even look around. 'Use this,' she said, tossing something over her shoulder. 'The ship's metal. Drum a tune. If you're lucky, it might sound something like a steel band.' She vanished into the wall.

Dana bent down and picked up her father's golf club.

114

It's just as well I'm never going to get back to Earth,
she thought as she held the gravitino gun over her
head and began to twirl it as fast as she could. *No one
would ever believe this anyway.*

'Whatever you do, don't blink, or you'll miss it,'
warned Liski Lup.

Liski was sitting at the main controls, dressed in
farmer's overalls, a red and white striped shirt, and
Maldox's golf cap. She liked to be comfortable when
she was piloting star ships. Dana was sitting beside
her in the co-pilot's seat, wrapped in a checked
blanket with a towel around her head and several
sleeping urds and her father's golf club on her lap.
She liked to dry off after a dip in melted anti-lac gel.
Dana and Liski were watching the pirates' shuttle
draw closer to the black hole, waiting for it to
disappear.

'I won't blink,' promised Dana, straining to keep
her eyes open. Even though there might never be
anyone human to tell her adventure to, she didn't
want to miss anything. Especially not something this
momentous. It wasn't every day that she successfully
completed a difficult intergalactic trouble-shooter
mission.

'There it goes!' cried Liski.

One nanosecond the shuttle was there, a tiny
silver point off starboard, and the next it was gone as
though it had never been.

'*There is only nothing, and everything is part of it,*'
intoned Liski Lup solemnly.

Dana looked over. 'What?'

115

'It's an old sensible Wadrickian saying,' explained Liski. 'We're very sentimental creatures, in our way.' She gave herself a shake.

'Well, you could have fooled me,' said Dana. 'You didn't seem very sentimental a few minutes ago. You haven't stopped laughing since I locked the pirates in the shuttle.'

Liski gunned the engines and turned the ship sharply to the left. 'I didn't say that we were overly sentimental like humans,' she said stiffly. 'I simply meant that we're sensitive.'

Dana sank back in her seat. She was feeling much better now that she was warm and safe and dry and not carrying on like a one-girl steel band. In fact, she was almost enjoying herself. Speeding through space when you were sitting at the helm of a starship and could see for miles was quite different to making the journey in a windowless cell. Dana had never imagined anything so vast or beautiful.

'So that's the end of Maldox the Merciless,' she said, hoping to show a little sensitivity of her own.

'For now,' said Liski as the ship ploughed through a glittering green particle cloud.

'What do you mean *for now*?'

Liski shook her head. 'What sort of physics do they teach you on Earth?' she asked. 'Everyone knows that what goes in comes out, even in a black hole.'

'You mean we went through all that trouble for nothing?' squeaked Dana. 'You mean Maldox will be back?'

'Don't you frown or feel too down, it'll be a while before he's around,' sang Liski Lup. 'But he always returns,'

she added. 'If there's one thing I know, I know what he's like. He comes from a very stubborn gene pool.' She pulled back on the throttle, smiling to herself. 'All in all,' she went on happily, 'I must admit that I did a splendid job.' She looped the spaceship between stars.

She did a splendid job? 'What about *me*?' protested Dana. 'You couldn't have done it without my help!'

Liski sniffed. 'Of course I could have.' The ship dipped and spun to the right. 'I just brought you along because I felt sorry for you, standing at the wrong bus stop like that because, as usual, you weren't paying attention.' She pointed a finger at Dana. She'd changed back to her gardening gloves. 'If it weren't for me you'd still be standing in the snow, waiting for the 77b. You're the one who should be thanking me.'

'Thanking you?' Dana wondered if this was how she'd spend the rest of her life, riding through the galaxies, arguing with Liski Lup. 'But I could have walked the plank. *And* I've lost my cello. I told you, my mother's still paying for that cello.'

'Then perhaps you should have learned to play it,' said Liski as they glided to a stop. She pulled up the handbrake. 'Here,' she said, reaching behind her and lifting Dana's old cello case from the floor. 'Maybe you can learn to play this.'

'What's that?' asked Dana. She'd thought the case was as gone as her cello.

Liski opened the case. 'Well, it's not a Beda-X Dematerializer, that's for sure,' she answered.

Dana stared. Inside the case was a musical instrument. It *looked* a lot like a cello, though not like any

117

cello Dana had ever seen. 'But it's got a red face,' said Dana. 'And a pick-up. And a lead.'

Liski gave her one of her vexed looks. 'What sort of electric cello would it be if it didn't have those things?' she wanted to know. She pressed a button and a doorway opened on Dana's left. 'You'd better hurry,' said Liski. 'You don't want to miss your supper.'

Dana turned to the open door. There, at the end of the familiar concrete path, was her house, covered with snow.

She turned back to Liski Lup. 'But—'

'Go on, now,' ordered Liski. 'Your mother's waiting.'

Dana looked through the doorway again just as her own front door opened and her mother switched on the outside light. Something made Dana glance at her watch. It said 5.48.

'Dana!' her mother called as Dana stepped from the ship. 'Where have you been? We were just about to start eating without you!'

Dana tucked her father's golf club under her arm and held her new electric cello tightly as she started to run. 'You won't believe it when I tell you,' she was shouting as she reached the house. 'But I've just had the most amazing adventure. See that spaceship out there?'

Dana's mother looked at her the way Liski Lup looked at her in a way that suggested that she couldn't believe her ears. 'Spaceship?' she repeated. 'What are you talking about? I just watched you get off the bus.'

Dana turned back to the kerb. The 77b was pulling away.

'I know you don't always pay attention,' said Dana's mother, 'but I should think you'd know when you'd been on a bus.'

Dana gazed out at the night. High over the opposite rooftops, a tiny speck, twinkling like a star, was disappearing into the sky. Knowing, somehow, that Liski Lup was watching her, Dana raised her hand and waved. *'You can't be sure just what you know, when you've been on a spaceship high and low,'* said Dana.